Cellius
Revenge

THE MYSTERY
OF THE
SILVER CUPS

BOOK 3

What People Are Saying About
Cellini's Revenge, The Trilogy

"I loved this trilogy and appreciated Bartlett's invitation to do a review as I am an older reader who, until recently, avoided fiction, but have loved the limited fiction to which I have become exposed. I guess these characters aren't real, but they quickly became real to me, like a friend or neighbor who experienced a very different physical, political, and cultural environment. The genealogy of the extended family was a softer, non-judgmental version of *Peyton Place*, with the continuing underlying mystery of the cups and Cellini's curse.

"I loved being able to take my time checking in with these characters who became my friends across the sea in Europe. Book Three, as well as the others, fit into my "good find" category, not only easy reading, but the kind you can readily pick up and put down, knowing your friends will be there when you get back - no hurry - you can pick me up and put me down without missing a beat or the intensity of the story. I was really sad when I realized I was done with this Alfred Hitchcock mystery of mysteries.

"A few men have asked me how their gender is represented. My response: Bartlett has done a wonderful non-judgmental portrayal of the single parent family with the parent being a father. Being the product of a single parent family with my own father, Bartlett's presentation of small-town men was 'warmly' real to me.

"Bartlett's description of relationships and the twist they can take, is so real one wants to read on or fall off a chair. I was sorry to say goodbye but will always remember the Cellini's cups, the world they came from and the world of the Evans family, from a small, English seaside town, and their exposure to those cups and how the cups impacted their lives. It was a good read. I recommend it for both young readers and older adults. Thank you, Wendy Bartlett, for adding your voice to my family library.
—Peggy Newgarden, PhD, University of Southern California, 1975

"A fascinating and ambitious mystery that unfolds over several centuries. It is an enjoyable and engaging story—highly recommended!"
—Joe Miller, writer, editor and award-winning banjo and guitar player

"Respect your curses,
for they are the instruments of your destiny."

—Joseph Campbell

Cellini's Revenge

THE MYSTERY OF THE SILVER CUPS

BOOK 3

WENDY BARTLETT

San Francisco Writers Conference Award Winner

Kensington Hill Books
Berkeley, California

Kensington Hill Books
Berkeley, California

kensingtonhillbooks.com

Cellini's Revenge: The Mystery of the Silver Cups—Book 3
/ Wendy Bartlett
ISBN 978-1-944907-18-1 print
ISBN 978-1-944907-19-8 ebook
Library of Congress Control Number: 2021922176

This book is dedicated to my two grandsons,
Leo and Charlie

ACKNOWLEDGMENTS

First and foremost, I would like to thank Laurie McLean for choosing me as the runner-up for the Fiction category in the 2007 San Francisco Writers Conference Writing Contest, which was started by two amazing, hard-working agents: Elizabeth Pomada and Michael Larsen.

I would like to acknowledge the following people for their very kind help and advice throughout the writing of *Cellini's Revenge, Book 2*: Joe Miller, the first editor of *Cellini's Revenge, Book 2* and Stefanie Reich-Silber for her sensitive editing from a British point of view. I especially want to thank Terri Sheldon for his historical British input, Leonard Pitt for his editing of the Paris chapter; Tom Gilb, Lindsey Brodie, Dean Curtis, Paul Lynch, Jane Glendinning and Beverly Tisdale for their varied and valuable input. I would especially like to thank Tyra Gilb for her excellent, sensitive artistic feedback on the colors for the three covers.

I would like to thank my writers' group for listening endlessly to this book and all my writing over many years: Dean Curtis, Joyce Scott, Marilynn Rowland, Sarita Berg, and Ruth Hanham. I would also like to thank Lindsey Brodie and Peggy Newgarden for their great suggestions.

I would like to thank Elizabeth Stark for her endless input along the way (and also for her suggestions regarding my blouse for my author photo), and her help with the great photographer, Angie Powers, whom I admire and thank so much for taking such an excellent and professional author photo of me and my dog, Timmy.

Last but not least, I want to thank and acknowledge the publishing guru, Ruth Schwartz, who has been a wonderful friend to work with, and who has helped me publish eight books, including this one, and we are working on a ninth.

THE PLANE–1987

Peter Evans, a detective who identified with Sherlock Holmes, a head above the crowd, felt a crick in his neck as he bent over his scribbled notes. Every day, he studied the movements of suspects–culprits–finding the plunder that surfaced. With his suspicious nature, he discovered the clues that kept him glued to his chosen profession.

Now that his newfound father, Michael Evans, was safely settled in with Peter's mother, Angela, the love of Michael's life, things had considerably quieted down.

Peter almost felt guilty that everything was finally running smoothly. At last, his teenage kids were old enough to fly to a music and language summer camp at a castle in the Austrian mountains. French and German phrases would be echoing up the staircase to the turret at the top of the castle called Schloss Leopoldstein; the best music and language teachers on the continent would teach his children French and German, spoken by other students who would be there from all over the world.

Peter bundled the children into the car and drove them to Gatwick Airport.

"Dad," said Cassandra, "You have to write!"

"I could phone you," he replied.

1

"No, we want letters. All the other children are going to get letters. We want real envelopes and please send photos–please, Dad!"

"Surely you should be sending me the photos?"

"No, we'll be homesick, so you have to send us letters and sweets, as well!"

"I can't promise you that, but I do promise you I'll send a letter and a photo. It'll be a surprise!"

They hurried themselves and their suitcases into the airport, and Peter kissed them each goodbye. Were they so independent now, his teenagers? How had that happened? He felt worried, and a little relieved to be free, followed by guilt at his own feelings about his newly found freedom.

Of course, he waited until the last moment when he knew they were going to be safely buckled in and ready to take off. He would stay there and then get into London to work on his latest case of a missing teenager. He began to go into his mind, despite the loudspeakers announcing gate changes, gate closures, slight delays.

This latest missing person puzzle was gradually coming into Peter's focus, the answer just out of reach. He loved this part of his career.

There was a loud noise from the runway. The loudspeaker announced a crash. Peter leaped up as he became aware and alarmed that it could possibly be the plane his children were on. He began running with other frantic, worried-looking people towards the information desk, which was already crowded with too many people, yelling, crying–probably parents whose own children were also on that plane.

ROME

Cellini galloped back from Florence to the Castle Sant'Angelo in Rome. As hastily agreed upon when escaping Rome the day before, his favorite apprentice pulled the huge gates of the castle open and shouted at him.

"Get inside, pronto, man!"

Cellini galloped his sweating horse through the gates and into the walled castle grounds. The gates crashed closed behind him, almost catching the exhausted horse's tail.

Cellini jumped from his horse, seeing that he was urgently needed up on the walkway of the castle. He leapt up the narrow stairs, drew his sword, and sliced off the head of a French soldier just climbing up onto the top of the wall. Cellini licked his lips. Here, for once, he could kill these invaders at will—no trial to endure later. The anger Cellini felt at this sack of Rome, without any warning, by King Francis 1 of France's massive hordes of soldiers, was enough to have Cellini lopping off heads with abandon. His deep pride as a Roman and a defender of the Church and the Pope was swelling up in his chest and had set his jaw for eternal vengeance.

"And you," he shouted, as a French soldier's head rolled by his feet. "And you," he shouted again, as his mighty sword chopped across the neck of another surprised soldier. "And you!" he growled at a third soldier.

Cellini's clothes were splattered with fresh warm blood, and he felt like a wolf with huge teeth, devouring his enemies.

ALIVE

Peter stretched his neck, hoping he could see higher above the jostling crowd in front of him. Where were his children? He jumped a few times, bumping a lady next to him.

"Sorry," he said.

Did they get out? Were they dead? He wanted to cry, to scream, to run! He saw the plane on its side, flames coming from the front. He saw the chutes and people sliding free. He felt his heart, which he feared had stopped.

"Oh, my God!" he said aloud.

Finally, Peter could just make out his own children in the distance, saw that they had survived. Henry was holding Cassandra's hand, and Oliver had grasped Henry's other hand. Was Oliver's face bleeding?

They were alive! It looked like so many had possibly died! He knew that so many probably choked on the smoke and fell down lifeless, while his children had probably squeezed through the crowd, pushing towards the chute. They carried nothing, just holding each other's hands and staggering away from the plane towards the other survivors, running and limping on the tarmac. Peter was frantic, but trying to be his best British self, his heart racing, his mouth dry, his bladder full, and his eyes searching every inch of his children in the distance for any limps or subtle shuffles.

How could this happen on a British plane, he wondered?

Peter and the other waiting people were informed that they would go into an emergency hall, which would require him and all the others to take a bus across the tarmac and wait in a long queue. His eyes never left the bus his children boarded. They clearly didn't see him. They probably didn't even know he was still in the airport. He checked constantly to see messages from the airline: two more hours?

"My poor children!" he said aloud. Well, they were hardly children now. But they were his children, and they were alive. He felt a guilty moment of sorrow for the ones who had not survived.

A flustered woman sitting next to him, searching her handbag, was sniffling and crying.

"Sorry!" he started. "I hope your family members made it out."

"Oh, yes. Thank God! That's the reason I'm crying!"

"I am pleased for you. Would you care for a handkerchief?" he asked, offering his embroidered handkerchief that had been a gift from his deceased wife, Jeannie.

As he handed it to her, he wondered if he should risk its loss. Peter watched the woman pat her tearful eyes and put it into her handbag as she scanned the tarmac. He would ask for its return later. Their concentration was on the survivors as they walked and limped together in a group towards the emergency hall.

Peter offered his hand towards the woman and said, "Peter Evans."

"Oh, sorry!" said the woman, her dark, long eyelashes burning into Peter's detective eyes in spite of her tears. "Susan Wilson," she said, her hand outstretched towards him.

"May I bother you to retrieve that handkerchief?" he stammered. "It was a gift from my late wife. Sorry!"

"Oh! Of course! Sorry!" She dug into her oversized handbag and took out the crumpled handkerchief.

It was the first time either of them had really looked into each other's faces.

"We know each other, don't we?" she asked, closing her handbag.

"I recognize you," said Peter. "I believe you live in Rottingdean, as well?"

"Oh, yes—yes," she spluttered. "My son Winston was on that plane. I saw him getting onto the bus, so he's okay," she said, adding, "I think our children go to the same school."

Peter's relief at sharing this tragedy was immense. No one else would ever understand. His three children had almost died. He wondered about her husband.

Peter and Susan were offered tea and biscuits, tables, and soft chairs, on which to wait for their children. They both glanced up regularly, like two birds awaiting an egg to hatch from the large automatic double doors, where their children would finally emerge.

By the time the two hours were up, he was just Peter, and she was just Susan. She had beautiful, dark brown eyes. By the time two hours and ten minutes were up, and the announcements blared like a ticking clock, each one had the email address of the other. People from the plane were finally emerging from the doors. As they watched the door like two expectant parents, Peter and Susan decided it might be best if they exchanged phone numbers.

The doors opened again, and his children ran or limped towards Peter, yelling, "Daddy, Daddy, Daddy!" They embraced in a big family hug and held on like they were stuck together with glue.

Peter glanced up and saw Susan running to her son, and her son was running to her. Then they all disappeared into a jumbled crowd of other passengers and relatives, hugging and kissing and crying. When Peter looked up from his tears, Susan was gone.

MEETING SUSAN

It was the sort of day that hints of winter, yet still has the lingering remains of fall, that brought Peter out into the world. It was a month since the accident. He checked his old-fashioned, comfy watch that had rested on his left wrist since his teens. His phone rested in his right front pocket. Half his brain waited for the ring tone.

Peter had finally found the time and courage to invite Susan out to have tea at his local café. He glanced from his watch, which said Susan was late, to the entrance to the café behind him, to where busy red buses were careening down the hill, scaring the bicyclists off the road.

Where was she? He checked his phone. No one had called. Should he call her? No, not yet. She was late for some good reason. He could wait. After another half-hour, he drew out his phone yet again. A cloud filtered across the sun with a frown. Nothing. He spied a bench and scuffled over to it and sat down. Jeannie had often been late–he'd learned patience in his marriage. He practiced it now, like it was an old friend.

And then, there she was, puffing over to him from the wrong side of the park. He stuffed his phone back into his pocket and produced a re-lieved smile.

"So sorry!" she spluttered and sat down at the other end of the bench.

"Not a problem," he lied, smiling.

There was an awkward silence. After all, they only had their children's disaster in common.

"It was Winston," she said as they got up and made their way to the café.

"Everything all right then?"

"Yes," she said. "Now it is."

"You?" he ventured.

"Oh, I'll be fine in a mo'," she said, lightly.

"Right," he said, dying to know, but desperate not to intrude. He felt like she was a magnet and he a lonely piece of metal.

"No, it's all right now, but it was touch and go there for a while."

"I see," Peter prodded, his eyebrows asking for further information.

"No, you don't, really. How could you?" She bit her nails. He waited, studying how, between the clouds, the sun was brightening up the red roses bursting forth among the browning leaves.

"Well, I must tell you. He has epilepsy and had a problem at school today. It only lasted a few minutes. I was on my way here and had to go right over to his school instead."

"Ah, now I do understand."

Her expression was thoughtful. "Yes. It starts, he falls to the floor, they put something in his mouth to protect his tongue, and then just as quickly, it's over and he's perfectly normal."

"I'm so sorry," Peter said, wondering what else he could say or do—wishing he could lay his hand upon her shoulder.

"By the time I arrived, he was back at his desk, working away at his maths just like the rest of the children."

Peter couldn't help it. "Was he born with this condition?"

She looked straight into his eyes. "It only started after the airplane accident."

Now Peter felt it was somehow his fault. Knowing that it was irrational, he accused himself anyway. The cloud covered the sun once again and the last red roses of fall darkened. Again, he longed to touch her, to cover her hand with his own, but just sat there instead.

At the end of their teatime, with the teapot emptied twice, they left the café. Peter stepped back and offered his hand. But his eyes would have given him away if she hadn't looked down. He wondered if he might embrace her gently one day soon. But Peter was a patient man. He had taken women out to pubs in London, but she was the most interesting woman he had met since Jeannie's death. He could not figure her out. Did she hold their handshake a little longer than usual? Did she finally look at him just after his eyes left hers? Did the warmth of her presence surround him, despite their not knowing each other very well?

"Thank you once again," she said, her large eyes looking at him longer than he had expected just then.

"My pleasure," he said, feeling too formal, and wondering if he had ever said those words before.

After a moment, she said goodbye, turned, and hurried away from the outside of their tiny café and over to the bus stop. Her son awaited her.

It wasn't exactly jealousy. A child, even a teenage child, was one's all. But Peter suddenly found that he longed to claim first place in her heart. Logically, he could never put her before his own children. Why would he wish for that place that he could never give to her himself? These relationships in later life were trouble: too much trouble. He waved to her. He was relieved to see that she paused, standing at the bus door, to glance and wave in her subtle way, almost like brushing a fly away from her face.

The following week, when Peter was helping Oliver out with homework, he heard a familiar ping. He checked his texts and found one from Susan Wilson. Would he and the children care to join her and her son for tea in three days?

"Remember Susan from the airport?" he ventured cautiously later that afternoon to his busy children.

"Sort of," said Oliver.

"She's invited us to tea on Friday!" said Peter. "Would you like to go?"

Oliver and Henry nodded, hardly looking up.

"Why not?" Cassandra muttered in a bored way.

After a short time, Peter, deep in thought about this upcoming tea, decided it was about time for bed.

"Bed!" he said, slamming his novel closed.

"Dad! It's early!" said Cassandra, lower lip out.

"Bed!" he said, sternly.

Peter had much to think about. This Susan was special. And he had three teenage children!

DINING

The whole family, Susan, and her son, sat at Susan Wilson's dining room table, overlooking the white-capped English Channel. There was, indeed, the obligatory teapot with its knitted tea cozy. On small blue Willow plates, she had placed whole wheat squares of sandwiches, along with the crust, tomato, and cucumber, topped with some brown Norwegian goats' cheese. There were small cakes of Greek baklava, and for the teens, there were chocolate oatmeal biscuits.

After the usual polite chatter, Peter couldn't help asking Susan where she had learned to eat Norwegian goats' cheese.

"I lived in Norway when I was twenty. I was there about six months, long enough to understand their jokes, which, sorry to say, did not match my own British sense of humor. Well, I sprained my ankle learning to ski, and was bored contemplating sitting indoors all winter. So, I left. "

"So, you came back to England in the winter?"

"Yes, as soon as I could hobble, I got on a train and came home. At least here I could venture out in the rain."

"Those were the days before planes caught fire," chimed in Cassandra.

Everybody shifted in their seats. Perhaps it was time to adjourn to the sitting room. Serviettes were dabbed on faces and placed on the table, chairs were pulled back with little scraping noises. There was a little coughing, and apologies for being in the way, and, of course, there were offers of help to clear off the table, along with protestations from Susan.

"Next time," insisted Peter.

Their eyes met–there would be a next time.

The view from the sitting room was broad, blue, wind-swept, and glorious.

"We live right up there at the top of Nevill Road," said Peter, pointing to the right.

"I know," Susan said.

"You know?" spluttered Peter.

"I've been there."

"You...."

"I knew Jeannie."

Peter put his hand over his opened mouth. His secrets were out– exposed. His hopes were dashed. He felt like he was sitting with Jeannie's spy, like Jeannie was laughing at him and his secret longings for Susan. Now his secret longings came to an abrupt halt.

"Our children played together," Susan said, nodding at Winston.

"I remember you!" Cassandra said to Susan.

Maybe it wasn't a conspiracy between Susan and Jeannie. The women in those days all seemed to blame men for everything.

Peter stopped chewing. He had had enough. All of a sudden, the idea of more entanglement made him almost want to vomit.

"I don't feel very well," he protested. "I didn't realize–I think we have to go."

"I am so sorry," Susan said. "I am so sorry for your loss. I read about it."

Enough. He really must escape. Would his misfortune follow him forever?

He stood up and made apologies, gathered his precious children, and walked up to their own house where he could hide in front of the fireplace and lick his psychic wounds.

THE MILLIONAIRE–1930

Sir Frederick Burrows, the renowned British millionaire, it was said, lowered the waterline of his sailboat in 1930, as it floated at the dock in Southampton, with small boxes of something very heavy.

Sir Frederick had donned his white sailor's cap to shade his straight, now sunburned nose, as well as his hearty beard and dark mustache, while he prepared to sail away to the South Pacific. His boat was laden with all his gold bricks and silver coins, and he was determined to get away from the Stock Market Crash that had ruined so many of his friends. He had planned this for years; he saw it coming, as his friends bought new cars and jewelry and danced the nights away. They laughed at him—in their polite way. After all, he was a knight—something about the First World War, a navy man.

Only one crew member joined him—a man from Ireland, Conor, who was very experienced as a sailor, and who Frederick, they said, trusted with his very life. He was young enough to do all the hard lifting and sail heaving, and old enough to be careful and thoughtful. He was an excellent galley cook—frying eggs, bacon, and fried potatoes that tasted first class, topped with a tin of tomatoes.

Sir Frederick Burrows didn't give a fig about his title. But he certainly did give a fig about his millions! He had held the newborn baby produced by his ex-wife only once. She told him it was over. What? How was that possible? She had just had the baby! But there was another man–another lucky one–still hanging on to his farm and his money, which he had stashed under the mattress. It was said he loved her, unlike Frederick–who did not.

His friends came to the docks to wish him well. They were all struggling by now, but nobody else was brave enough to set sail for the South Pacific. They preferred the known, however frightening they now found it.

Conor got to work, tearing the labelled paper off each of the tins and marking them with ink: peas, carrots, berries, chicken soup, barley, beans, and Carnation Evaporated Milk. No sea water would wash those labels away. It was nice to know what you might be eating before you blindly opened the tin! Plenty of variety to mix with the fish they intended to catch in the middle of the ocean. He then stacked the many tins of food along the shelves and finished up stowing the gold bricks under the floorboards. He shut the hatch and locked it.

As they sailed away and old friends waved and waved, Frederick wondered what would become of his friends. He wondered what would become of his baby son, but he had taken care of that in his way. He didn't care what would become of his ex-wife–not a flying fig. He would never pay her a penny of his hard-won money–not that she cared now. He had never really loved her–not that he could remember. So, good riddance to her! Maybe one day he would shake the hand of his son. But Sir Frederick intended to be gone for the rest of his life, so that would probably never happen. He kept remembering the paintings of the Tahitian women now so popular, painted by Gauguin. Perhaps there was a woman in the South Pacific who would appreciate him, not even noticing his wealth. Well, she might notice his lovely yacht. She might. He could dream. He was, indeed, a dreamer. He waved. They waved. He turned his face away now. As Conor pulled up the mainsail, the breeze took up the slack, the sail ruffled and ballooned, and Frederick cut the engine.

He smiled. He had won something. He'd won! He was free!

PROMISE OF CUDDLES—1987

Peter had tried to push Susan into the back of his mind, but he knew that he really liked her, and that his memory of Jeannie should really have nothing to do with Susan. He braced himself and made the call to invite her to tea at the local café.

They met outside the café. It was small inside, but not so small that Peter and Susan's conversation would be noticed.

Peter wondered that if he kept his hand on hers, even a millisecond longer, she might pull hers away. He lifted it as their eyes met, and her eyes said, "That's enough for now." They looked towards the window, the door, and the other people.

"Let's go for a walk," Peter suggested after they had finished their tea. Susan looked relieved and began gathering her handbag and jacket in a slightly hurried fashion. Perhaps he had misread her. Perhaps he was only a momentary distraction for her between her son's epileptic seizures. Her smile wasn't a real smile. It was a tortured smile. Perhaps this would be a short walk? She lived just a little too far from town to run into by chance in the future.

"Sorry," she said, bumping into someone busy reading a book. "Sorry," she repeated, but with his earphones, her protestations were wasted.

The people in the café all seemed to look up with irritated faces. Peter held out his hand so she could gracefully squeeze by without bumping anyone else. She took it. He almost hoped she would trip and fall so he could rescue her in his lonely arms, given that these days he was touched only by his children's brief hugs, which were reserved for inside the house. After all, one of the children's friends might see. His children were on their way. They didn't have epilepsy, like Susan's child, and, one-by-one, his children would leave for university.

Susan let go of his hand immediately. He thought to himself–*Women!* Then he caught his old-fashioned internal rhetoric and realized, when he thought back on Helen's therapy, that his own hurt could easily have been called–*Men!* At the café door, he stepped back and gestured for her to leave first. He questioned this as old-fashioned behavior, but surely it would be rude if he didn't let her go first? Would he appear to be a knight or a male chauvinist? How long could he endure performing this politically correct behavior?

His wife, Jeannie, had been a harsh teacher. Were all women like that? He hadn't really dated that much for so long; he'd had no opportunity to catch up. He heard about dating sites, but the thought of them made him very uncomfortable. As she passed in front of him, he smelled a dainty whiff of her perfume. His nostrils flamed. His heart thumped. Had she intentionally put out the scent of an interested woman? His puppy dog paws leapt up, his tongue hanging out, panting. He held the door open for her, and smelled that perfume again, as she whisked by him. He followed her. To him she was twenty-five and not the mother of a son with epilepsy. She was a promise of warmth, cuddles, intimate talks, and bodily satisfactions. How he longed to reach out, one more time, to take her hand while they walked side-by-side, up the hill to the bluff and the sea, and the hope of a future, as they shared the view across the channel.

TIME TO INVITE SUSAN

Later in the week, Peter decided he might invite Susan to his house for a dinner party with the family. When the day arrived, he was excited and anxious, happy that Cassandra and Henry, at least, were scuttling around, laying the table and adding chairs.

Susan came a little late. They all sat around the table, and, at last, Oliver came into his own as a waiter. When all the plates were filled and served, Oliver tripped at the last minute and fell down, throwing his own plate across the room.

"No, no! Not to worry," he said. He cleaned it up, served another dish of food for himself, and walked slowly to his place, sitting down with a satisfied smile.

Peter looked around at them all: Michael, Angela, Cassandra, Henry, Oliver, and dear Susan and Winston.

"It's probably all about the silver cups," Cassandra started. "Oliver tripping...."

Peter didn't want to tell Susan about the cups, yet there she sat, eyes wide, while Cassandra spilled the beans. He had planned this as a private conversation at some future point, when Susan might possibly be more committed to this family. No good scaring her off, was there?

Peter gave Cassandra a dirty look, which she obviously missed, as she was watching Susan's fork stop halfway up to her mouth.

"What cups?" asked Susan.

"Hasn't Peter told you about the silver cups?" asked Oliver.

"I'd rather leave that for now, if you don't mind," said Peter, stepping on Oliver's shoe under the table.

Henry said, "It's all a bunch of superstitious rubbish, if you want my opinion."

"Good, that's all we need to say, then, isn't it?" Peter said, glaring at Cassandra.

"It's just a silly thing. We have no problem talking about it, though, do we?" Cassandra said to Michael.

"I should say not!" said Michael, his mouth rather full.

"Don't spoil Susan's dinner," said Angela.

"No, no!" said Susan. "Nothing could spoil my dinner. Please go ahead. I'm all ears."

"Good food," Peter said, hoping to change the subject.

"They're my cups!" said Michael.

"Here we go," said Oliver. Another tap on his shoe.

"Not now, dear," Angela said to Michael.

"I found them in a bag of rubbishy items on the back of the cart of a rag-and-bone man, didn't I?" said Michael. "...in the 40s," he added.

"...with David," said Angela.

"Well, yes, David was there, wasn't he?" said Michael. "But I pulled them out of the bag, so they were mine!"

"Who's David?" asked Susan.

"That's my brother," said Michael.

"...who died tragically," said Oliver. Peter's shoe hovered over Oliver's toe underneath the table.

"Yes, well, can we all talk about that another time?" suggested Peter.

"Peter had two fathers," blurted Oliver.

Susan looked at Peter.

"Not really," Peter tried.

She kept looking at him.

"Well, we can talk about that on another occasion," Peter said, grabbing his wine glass and saying, "Here's to Michael, my father!"

Everyone raised a glass and said, "Cheers! To Michael, Peter's father!"

"And what about David, his other father?" said Oliver.

"Other father?" asked Susan.

"Another day, please!" said Peter.

"Yes, all right, but what about the silver cups?" asked Susan.

"They're in Italy," said Henry.

"…where they belong," said Oliver.

"Catherine gave hers back," said Cassandra.

"Who's Catherine?" asked Susan, finally taking her bite.

"She found the cups buried right under Grandma's back deck," said Cassandra.

"But the Italians insisted she give them back to Italy," said Henry.

"…or they wouldn't let her leave England," said Oliver.

"American," added Peter, into Susan's ear.

"Oh, I see," said Susan, politely.

All Peter feared now was that they might start talking about the curse on their family.

"They're bad luck!" said Cassandra.

"Really?" asked Susan.

"Bloody superstition, I'd say," said Henry.

"Shall we have our dessert?" said Peter, still hoping to alter this conversation.

"But why are they bad luck?" asked Susan.

Peter stood up and made rather a lot of noise while clearing the plates.

"It was probably a bad luck curse of Cellini's for anybody who owned them, until they were returned to Italy," said Michael. "Anyway, I'll never forgive Catherine for that! They were mine!"

"She had to give her cups up, same as you, Michael," said Angela.

Peter only hoped Susan would ask for her sweet.

"Ah! Bad luck. Where are they now?" she asked.

"Italy," said Peter. "What would you like for dessert?"

"No choice–vanilla ice cream," said Oliver, jumping up to serve it.

Peter smiled at his party, all expecting ice cream, and hoped that somebody might change the subject immediately.

A week later, Peter invited Susan to have tea at his house. He wanted to see her again in his family setting. They all sat in the kitchen around Peter's large, long, wooden pine table. He wasn't surprised to hear Cassandra ask Michael about his story of the Cellini cups.

"Grandpa," said Cassandra. "Tell us about what happened to your six silver cups!"

Michael looked up, apparently delighted to be called Grandpa, and had no qualms about repeating his famous story.

"Well, all right," he began. "There I was, happily sitting with Catherine in the restaurant, you know, David's wife, well, sort of, wife…."

"…they never got married," Cassandra said to the table of family listeners.

"We know," said Oliver.

"Right," said Michael. "As we all remember, David had married our Angela to give our Peter his name…."

"…Evans." said Cassandra.

"Shh," said Henry.

"And she and I moved here to David and Catherine's house," said Peter.

"…because Catherine was in jail anyway for twelve years, wasn't she," said Cassandra, adding, "…and anyway, they never married, so Angela got the house. Legal wife, etc., etc., etc."

"Correct," said Michael. "Where was I?"

"More scones?" asked Angela.

"Shhh," said Henry. "Oh, sorry, Grandma."

"So, as you all know, but I am happy to repeat it," said Michael, "I was taken from a perfectly pleasant luncheon with Catherine to let her know…."

"…that you were the silent Mr. Smith when she was in jail," said Oliver.

"Exactly," continued Michael.

"And along came those MI5 agents, grabbed my shoes, and dragged me off to jail!"

"Booo!" yelled everybody.

"Exactly. And there I was," said Michael, "not able to have my lunch (I was really hungry) and not able to really explain the situation to poor, astonished Catherine."

"Booo!" the group shouted.

"Would you believe it?" he said.

"Nooo!" said the group "That those bugg…uh…blinders went to my flat and stole my six silver cups from behind my suits in my closet…."

"…poor hiding place!" said Henry.

"Yes, well, now I see that, of course, but they ransacked my whole flat…the blinders, and when I got home, I couldn't believe it. Those cups were mine!" he said in an elevated tone. "I found them!"

"We all know you found them with David," said Angela.

"But they really belonged to Italy, right?" said Cassandra.

"Those Italians have them now, I've heard. I'll never get over it. But I'm free, thanks to Catherine's brilliant lie in court, (bless her), and I'm here to tell the tale, and not in some smelly jail!"

"Yay!" everybody shouted.

"Shhh!" said Angela.

"Yay!" shouted Michael, and everybody, including Angela, yelled, "Yay!"

Everybody looked at Susan. Peter was pleased to see her shouting, "Yay!" along with everybody else.

CELLINI'S SECOND TRIP

Cellini opened his cracked palms and saw the story of a lifetime of hard work, endless nights by candlelight, burns on hands that loved their chosen work. His hands looked like he was old, but, in fact, he was only in his mid-forties. Yet his artistic life had begun practically with his birth.

As he prepared his second trip to the d'Este Villa, after so many years, he remembered how much larger the Villa had become since his attempt to deliver the twelve silver cups so many years before. Of course, it had always been huge and very grand, having been built over old Roman ruins and then extended later on from an old monastery site. But d'Este was a man who liked art and loved opulence. Luckily, d'Este had excellent taste, as did his aunt before him, who particularly liked to procure large paintings of grand, wealthy persons for the Villa around 1500, before d'Este inherited it.

D'Este's specialty was statues, both in his vast gardens with the hundred fountains, and within the long, high-ceilinged, ornate halls of the mansion—also lined with tall oil paintings of wealthy and famous men.

Cellini and the Cardinal had designed the ornate gold and enamel salt cellar much earlier. It was created from the models they made, and years later, d'Este saw that it went to the King of France. The large, decorative silver cup that Cellini was to present to d'Este had an echo of the ornate figures around the silver masterpiece that balanced the salt cellar and were inspired by the hard labor that was going into the salt cellar. It was almost like a race to Cellini, and the cup was the winner. D'Este, the Cardinal of Ferrara, would be pleased to have this excellent cup to show off, while King Francis I of France enjoyed the salt cellar.

"What do you think?" Cellini asked Francisco, who had come to visit and witness the completed cup before Cellini left.

"Better than the salt cellar in its unique way," replied his lifelong friend.

Cellini smiled and pulled his beard with extreme pride. He'd done it! He'd made a gift that no other cardinal could come close to owning. The King of France could keep his lovely salt cellar, for it was the most excellent piece of silver any king might want to have on his long, exquisitely laid out dining table, with, perhaps, kings and queens sitting and eating while marveling at this exquisite piece. It was almost finished. But first Cellini would deliver his completed cup with his own worn hands.

"Excellent!" said Francisco.

"I have to agree!" laughed Cellini.

RIVOLI–1546

Cellini remembered the old road he had taken so many years earlier, the first time he tried to deliver the cups back in 1527. This time, he led the Cardinal d'Este's soldiers through what looked like the very road he had used. None of the soldiers contradicted him, so he led them on. He knew they had just traveled along a faster, nearby route, on their way to meet him and to escort him safely back to the Cardinal's Villa in Rivoli.

On the way to Rivoli, the only detour along this route was through the old village, where Cellini's cups had been stolen. The new road there was still just one lane wide, but on higher ground, with less mud clogging up the horses' hooves. Cellini insisted on going through it, if only to frighten the villagers into coughing up his twelve stolen silver cups.

Cellini knew he would be returning from the d'Este mansion with only his manservant, Marco, and not the d'Este's soldiers, and he would be stopping in that small village to water the horses. He had wanted to warn the villagers, in advance, by the presence of the soldiers, that he still had the support of Cardinal d'Este–in case they wanted to cause trouble to Marco and himself.

The journey had lasted two nights and three days from Florence to Rivoli.

In the village, on the way back home to Florence, Cellini, turning his head, noticed a very old man and his very old horse and cart, accompanied by another middle-aged man. He couldn't help thinking they both had lowered their heads when they passed him, as if to hide their faces. Cellini thought, for a fleeting moment, that they could have stolen the cups, but dismissed it immediately, knowing they were too slow-going to make a getaway. Still, Cellini felt a sense of discomfort after he and Marco mounted their horses and galloped past them. Somehow, they reminded him of a similar horse and cart he thought had sped by towards the port all those years ago. Surely, the cups had not been taken onto that galleon and into the open sea–that galleon that might have sailed from Italy, never to return. It was only a hunch. He dismissed the thought at once. It was a long time ago, and he still needed to return to Florence and put the finishing touches on his amazing salt cellar.

SOMETHING HAD CHANGED

Peter's home office was leaking in the corner. He fiddled with his papers. His computer was slow: the printer kept jamming. The rain outside was thundering upon the roof. He worried about making his mortgage payments.

Cassandra was being silent again. Henry had lost his summer job, and Oliver had been staying out too late. Peter worried about the cost of living. He struggled over the paperwork for Henry's university entrance applications. The only positive thing for Peter was that there were plenty of detective assignments, with so many more desperate people trying to outwit, outdo, underpay, steal, borrow forever and sign bad checks, that he had enough work to keep all his own payments going.

There was that single mom, who had stolen her ex-husband's car, and then taken off for France. There was the drug addict who stole mail from people's mailboxes and cashed their checks. There was an unsolved break-in where the people asleep in the house ended up dying of gas poisoning. But mostly, it all seemed to be related to people's inability to keep up with the mysterious rising of their debt, and their inability to balance their income and expenses. That's what Peter figured was the bottom line, but he admitted to himself that he knew nothing about finances, and couldn't point the dirty finger, even though he was managing well enough, considering.

Peter was called into court about once a week, usually on a couple of leftover London cases that had dragged on for years. He hardly had a moment to think about women. But more and more, the faces of both his ex-therapist Helen and his friend Susan surfaced; he imagined intimacy with each one that he—in reality—didn't feel he had time for. A walk in the park and a bite of lunch somewhere was about his limit. Besides, he couldn't decide between them. So, he hunkered down over his computer and his files and wished he could do more in his every endeavor.

Tonight, he planned to have another talk with Cassandra, who spent most of her time in her room. Henry and Oliver stayed out as late as tolerable, even in the rain. Peter felt an ache somewhere deep down for some adult conversation—silly things even, like the leak in the roof. A partner would listen. Who else had the time or patience when his roof was leaking? One good thing was the pub, where men could go and complain about their house problems, but Peter wasn't a drinker, and saw all too often what happened to families where the pub won.

The table was laid for the four of them, a little family holding fast to their teacups and glancing longingly at the new television, which was not allowed to be on during suppertime.

Henry was making plans for university and had a new girlfriend, who was definitely going to Sussex University in the fall. Cassandra would have preferred to be on a picnic with her now firmly rooted boyfriend, Gerald. Oliver was captain of the school cricket team and obviously wished he were having supper anywhere else.

Peter, meanwhile, was working on several cases that involved trips to London to the MI5 about suspicious sailboats arriving on the coast from Europe. And secretly, he kept his eye on Angela and Michael.

Part of Peter was still eager to move on from Rottingdean. He had even approached Michael about letting the house to him on Pond Street in Hampstead, where Angela and Peter had lived when Peter was a young lad. But Michael reminded Peter that the tenants had rights for two more years. Peter thought that would be perfect. Once the children had flown, he would move back to Hampstead. He had two years to find out if one of those two lovely women was willing to relocate with him.

Peter started on the sausages, eggs, and potatoes; Cassandra took over and finished them. They all arrived at the table at exactly 6:30 p.m. as usual.

"I'll serve," said Oliver, reaching for the large hot iron skillet.

"Thank you, Oliver," Cassandra said. "Dad, he's growing up!"

"We all grow up in our own time, and Oliver's no different. Well done, Oliver!" said Peter, patting Oliver on the back.

Oliver gave his crooked smile with a twinkle in his eyes. "It's not like I never served before!" he said.

Henry and Cassandra muffled their giggles, and Cassandra raised her eyebrows.

Cassandra said, "I wouldn't mind a compliment, Dad. I've been slogging away here for years without a thank you!"

"I thank you all the time!" protested Peter.

"But it isn't special, is it?" pouted Cassandra.

Peter could see an escalation brewing. Sibling rivalry was rampant, as always. He mused at the number of people in his field of work who bashed each other up who were siblings.

"Enough!" he said, trying to stop further protests.

Henry, who was old enough now, said, "Dad never complimented me, and I did all the work the whole year after Mum died!"

"Henry, that was a hard time," said Peter. "You did well."

"I was too young," said Cassandra.

"Me, too!" said Oliver.

"Me, too," said Peter.

They all laughed and began to eat.

A YEAR OFF

Cassandra was now a young lady who apparently knew better than Peter what she wanted, while he was the one who really knew what she needed. Some days later, as they were driving down the hill from their house, Cassandra said she wanted to take a year off school as a gap year before entering university.

"Take a year off?" Peter spluttered.

"Oh, Dad! Everybody is doing it these days. It's not like there's a war and no money to spare. It's also an education, isn't it?"

"But you got a grant! Will they cancel it?"

"Of course not," she answered rather slowly. "At least, I wouldn't think so."

Peter thought of his earning power. He thought of his dwindling savings and how he'd hoped she would get a summer job as her brothers had. He thought of his mortgage and his second mortgage and the increasing interest rate.

But he smiled at her and said, "We can't predict the future, can we? I think you could take a gap year, but first you have to do a bit of research and find out if the grant will still be available next year. I'm not a millionaire, you know!"

"Oh, Dad! Of course, I will!"

Cassandra giggled in her seat and gazed out at the pointed rooftops and the puffy white clouds.

Peter turned the car right onto High Street. Cassandra started waving frantically and yelling.

"Stop, Dad! I need to get out. See you back at the house."

Peter pulled over, and she leapt out and ran over to Gerald. Peter saw them jumping up and down through his side mirror. Did they have a travel plan she had not mentioned to him? He felt a lonely moment, with the children slipping out of his grasp and into their own lives. He was not in control, and he didn't like it at all. But he was also realistic. He'd had his own youth and mistakes. That helped him let them go. It was a new time to be a teenager. Still, it somehow seemed beyond his under-standing.

As he pulled into the traffic, he noticed them holding hands. Her boyfriend seemed genuine enough. Peter looked ahead and wondered where the next chapter of his own life might lead him. He didn't fancy being the caretaker of his aging parents.

And there they were, right ahead of him: Angela with Michael, who was pulling a wicker shopping cart, just coming out of Sainsbury's. Angela held his other arm. They looked happy enough together. Peter sighed. If only he had done something differently in his marriage to Jeannie, he might have a wife still on his arm. Then he thought of Jeannie. No, she would never have held his arm.

Then he mused about his ex-therapist Helen, and then he thought of Susan. Which one would hold his arm? And which one would happily transfer to live in Hampstead with him? Perhaps neither. Perhaps he would have to strike out on his own. He would find a woman somehow. Perhaps she already lived in London.

THE USUAL CAFÉ

When Cassandra came home one evening later that week, a box of Tampax fell out of her purse. Peter looked away and didn't say anything, but his relief that she was not pregnant was palpable. He figured he was free from inevitable thoughts of abortion, or of being a grandfather, and that he was free to phone Susan.

It had been a while since Peter had seen Susan. And Helen had insisted, yet again, that he and she were "just friends."

Peter missed Susan. Of course, he'd been so busy lately with his investigations. Things developed so quickly with the possibilities of not only DNA, but now the Internet. He felt like he was constantly traveling from Rottingdean to London and back. The only times he had to himself were the train rides when he caught up on the news.

But now there was a lull, and he needed the warm smile of a woman, the feeling he could drop the pretense of being a strong, single parent. He needed someone who was soft and non-judgmental. After all, she had a child, too. Peter wondered how her son's seizures were going. Perhaps they had subsided with time. But the poor guy had had such a traumatic time after the plane accident.

Peter was guiltily grateful his own children had come through with not so much as a scratch. True, the idea of flying no longer appealed to them, but mostly they just got on with their lives.

He dialed. His mind was busy with a thought about how stupid criminals could be, like they almost wanted to go back to jail, when Susan answered.

"Hello?"

"Susan! It's Peter. Sorry! It's been a while. I'm hoping you are well." Peter was shaking involuntarily.

"Oh, Peter! How lovely to hear your voice!"

Peter breathed gently and remembered now how good her voice made him feel.

"I was hoping you might have time…."

"Let's meet in the usual café," she suggested before he could finish his sentence.

"How about later today?" he said, almost interrupting her.

Peter felt like kissing her and swore to himself he would if he got a chance.

"About four-thirty, then?" she said.

"That would be lovely," he answered.

Peter wanted to ask if she would have to run off to her son, but he was mostly pleased that they might continue their friendship—once again.

He couldn't help it; he made his way to the café early and hovered outside. It was a fine day with a slight breeze from the sea. He watched the fluffy clouds sail by, soaking up the sun as they departed. Spring was in the air. Those stupid criminals would be planning more purse snatching and carjackings, but right now Peter couldn't care less. Life was grand. He breathed in that fresh sea air and was glad to be alive.

And there she was, alighting from the bus.

Peter looked directly into her eyes from a distance. She was looking back into his eyes in a way that felt to Peter like they had more to say to each other, and once they sat down in the café and had ordered their tea, neither could stop talking.

ONE MORE ADVENTURE

Susan was beautiful, soft, and loving; he felt his love for her growing. It was like he looked behind him apologetically to an invisible Helen, but kept on going forwards, towards the cementing of this satisfying relationship with Susan. He remembered how the children had told Susan about the silver cups and the bad luck they suspected they had all experienced as a result of owning them for so long.

After some weeks of seeing Susan more regularly, Peter thought that, perhaps, it was time now to have tea again with Angela and Michael. Just two days before, Susan had said she would love to travel to the continent with Peter. Soon, she had said. Peter was thrilled. Now, he needed to get some reassurance from Michael and Angela that they would take care of the children.

"They're a nice, settled couple now," he reassured Susan, but more, himself.

"Yes, I thought so," said Susan.

Peter relied on them being middle-aged. They might possibly behave themselves out of the sheer exhaustion of pretending to be younger. They had settled into a routine now, and Angela had said their life was almost boring. She had sighed, but perhaps a desire for one more adventure—just one more—simmered beneath that sigh. Her health was good, she'd said, as was Michael's. Everything worked just fine! Peter laughed with her at that comment.

Some days later, as the four of them sat in Angela's sitting room, Peter was secretly hoping their hips would falter and he could feel the relief of knowing they would not dare go off to the continent again. But there was a dangerous twinkle in Angela's eyes as she winked at Michael. Susan sat quietly.

Peter was not a detective who missed cues. "Okay. Where are you going, you two?"

"Peter! We never said!" Angela protested innocently.

"I saw you wink at Michael!"

"No. Just something in my eye."

Peter knew full well when his mother was lying. "Mum. Come off it. What's the plan?"

"No plan–right Michael?"

"No plan at all," Michael echoed.

They both sipped their tea.

"Good," said Peter, "because I was hoping you'd take the children for two weeks. Susan and I are going abroad." He smiled at Susan, who was obviously trying to be invisible.

"When are you going?" asked Angela, alarm in her voice.

"In a fortnight," said Peter.

Angela and Michael looked horror stricken, like their own plans had just fallen flat.

"Of course, we will!" said Angela. Michael gave her a look of disappointment.

Peter knew what was going on. He reached over to lay his hand lightly on Susan's. She smiled at him.

"You go along, you two," said Angela. "We'll manage, won't we, Michael, my love?"

"Of course. They're my grandchildren," said Michael. "It'll be really good–really good. We could take them somewhere nice, Angela, couldn't we?"

Peter squinted at the pair of them. Were they silently planning to take them along on their own trip?

"Oh!" said Peter. "Where will you take them?"

He didn't have to wait long. To his enormous relief, they said they planned to take them on a day trip to Arundel Castle.

WOULD IT BE FINE?

Peter sat in a funk, wondering where Angela and Michael had really planned to take his children–rather, their grandchildren–as they were fond of reminding Peter. Of course, they would tell him–wouldn't they?

Peter began to worry that they would tell him a lie and take them somewhere else instead. He had hoped they would go visit Stonehenge or some of those wonderful ancient castles on the south coast. But the last thing Peter imagined was a trip abroad. It was so easy now with that Chunnel by train or car. It was no longer necessary to take a ferry, which only made you seasick right at the beginning of your journey.

He tried to invite them to tea at his house, for once.

"I prefer our house, if you don't mind, Peter," said Michael.

"Oh, really? Are you sure you are up to taking the children on a journey?" he asked lightly. "It just seems better to sit here with the ocean view, don't you think, Father?"

"Love this view," agreed Michael.

Peter felt they somehow had more power over him in their own house, which, he mused, used to be his own house. Never mind. He agreed that they would all meet at Angela and Michael's house.

Henry was late, but the traffic along the coastal highway was worse than usual–some accident, he claimed.

Angela had provided an array of sweet croissants and some delicious fluffy cake she had baked. Bribery!

The children and Peter entered the house and immediately joined Michael and Angela around the coffee table, making "yum-yum" sounds until Peter felt it was time to get down to business.

"So," he said, definitively.

Everybody looked at him, licking the crumbs and jam off their lips. It was like he was the only one interested in why they were there in the first place.

"So," he said, again. "Good cake, Mum."

Angela smiled, like she had accomplished a big plan. Maybe she had. Peter bit his lip, waiting for the bombshell.

"If you must push the subject, Peter," she said, "We have tickets to Paris."

"Paris?" Peter exclaimed. "Why so far? What about all the history right here in England?" Surely, that would keep them from going to France!

"England?" said Oliver, "That's no fun!"

"Oliver!" scolded Peter.

"France is romantic," said Cassandra. "We've studied all about it at school."

"Then you don't have to go there, do you?" Peter said, knowing he'd already lost the battle. But this was a new era. "Alright, then," Peter gulped. "But I insist on a daily phone call to be sure they are safe."

"Dad! We're not children anymore!" protested Henry.

"Yes, but I am still your father and only parent. I will worry, won't I?"

Angela and Michael shot each other a smile.

Peter wanted to time his and Susan's trip to Italy with their trip to Paris. Susan had agreed to go, but she only had certain free dates.

Apparently, Angela and Michael had already booked all their train tickets from Saint Pancras.

It would be fine. It really would, wouldn't it?

But by the day of their departure, Angela had developed a bad cold, and Michael immediately began sneezing heartily, so Peter and Susan, very reluctantly, decided they would have to postpone their own trip.

DOOR AJAR

Some weeks later, Peter wandered along up High Street, his back to the sea. Fish and chips were settling into his stomach as he stopped at the greengrocer's, admiring the colors of the fruit—the yellows and oranges and reds and greens—their own dance of living. Jeannie had loved those colors. Perhaps within him, Jeannie was also admiring those shades and shadows and delicate changes as the sun passed over them? Would it ever end? Could he truly love another while his heart was broken and his dreams were nightmares?

The wind swept up High Street, laughing and complaining, and letting the pedestrians know who their ultimate boss was. Peter ordered a large bag of apples and oranges despite the climb ahead up the street towards home.

"Lovely day," smiled the greengrocer.

"It was!" Peter said, noting the wind banging a sign just next door, with a noise like a warning.

He paid, nodded, and said, "Cheerio, then," to the grocer, turning and almost leaning forward and continuing home, ready to be the jolly father he wanted his children to remember.

When he got home, he was startled to see the front door ajar. Perhaps he or the children had forgotten to pull it tight? It was a stubborn old door now, yelling for attention at regular intervals. Peter's carpentry skills were minimal. He groaned. He paused to look about the front hedges and the gate.

Peter stepped into the house. The last thing he remembered was the sight of the coat rack crashing to the floor–and then nothing. When he awoke, jumbled up amid the winter coats, he felt his forehead. His hand was now bloody. He grabbed his handkerchief and mopped his brow. He struggled to stand up, feeling slightly dizzy, and staggered into the kitchen. The whole house had been turned upside down. His children were tied to chairs and blindfolded, and every drawer in the kitchen was on the floor with utensils scattered around them. He ran to his children, so big now, and tore off their blindfolds and started to untie their hands and feet.

"What happened?" he spluttered.

"Daddy!" sobbed Cassandra.

"Burglars?" Peter asked, hoping it was only burglars.

"It looks like they didn't take anything, and they didn't hurt us, really," said Henry.

"What did they look like?" Peter asked, involuntarily making fists.

"Italians," said Henry.

"Italians?" Peter breathed.

"Yes," said Oliver.

"Are you sure?"

"Yes. We heard them talking in Italian," said Henry.

"Italians," Peter mumbled to himself as he finished unbinding his children's wrists and rubbing them.

"Let's at least have tea," he said then, picking up the kettle from the floor and filling it with water.

He shuffled around, picking up knives, forks, and spoons with one hand, and holding his forehead with the other. "Why would they leave with nothing?" he muttered to himself.

He felt tears welling up, despite his willpower.

"Italians…." he muttered.

"I'll bet it's to do with those Italian silver cups!" ventured Oliver.

Peter had just had that flashing thought and dismissed it as impossible. He stopped and stared into the distance, into the past, into that impossible time.

"What were they looking for?" asked Henry.

"I don't know." Peter tossed the thin ropes from Cassandra's arm across the room. "I can't believe this!"

"Dad, you're bleeding!" said Cassandra, leaping up to the sink and the paper towels. She drenched them in water, then dabbed his puzzled brow.

"I've missed something," mumbled his detective voice, allowing himself to be tended to.

"You always say that!" said Cassandra.

"Do I?" he asked, reaching out and taking the towel from Cassandra and holding it to his forehead.

Henry got up and walked to the back door. It was standing ajar. Peter walked over to him, and they both stared out at the sea as if its tumbling mass could provide the answers.

"Things have been going along very nicely these last few years. Is this just a coincidence? Is this random? What have I missed?"

Cassandra came over to Peter and he put her arm around his shoulder while Henry lightly touched Peter's arm. The ocean stared back, with Italy somewhere in the distance around the curve of the earth, tantalizing them all.

Cassandra went outside to pick up the newspaper.

"Silver Cups Missing!" Cassandra read aloud.

"Suspect: An Englishman," she read.

"Dad! You?"

"I didn't do a thing!" he spluttered. "I've been in England the whole time. This is insane!"

"Did you want them back that much?" asked Henry.

"Don't be foolish!" Peter stammered. "All they were was bad luck!" He smacked his forehead, as usual, but groaned at the sting of his wound. "Looks like I have my new case. I'll call the police, right now!"

"Do you think you should?" asked Oliver.

"Of course, I should!" Peter said, his voice a little high-pitched.

"Dad," Cassandra said, slowly.

"Yes," Peter said, equally slowly.

"Where have our grandparents gone for their anniversary?"

"Italy...." he answered.

They all groaned.

"Don't call the police yet, Dad," said Henry.

Peter looked at his hands and imagined them tied by a laughing jester with a thin, invisible rope.

THE PHONE CALL

Images of Peter's father, Michael Evans, and his mother, Angela Evans, now holidaying in Italy, were clouded over by images of this middle-aged couple distracting the museum guard long enough to stash the Cellini cups into Michael's backpack. Every night Peter woke up with a new nightmare, a scenario where he was the detective questioning the guards and the museum staff, getting halting, unintelligible answers with an Italian accent.

"Where were you standing when…." or "Did you see anything out of the ordinary?" And then, "Here, standing just here!" And the face was blotted out—then peering closer, looking like the devil himself with an eerie smile.

Peter awoke in a sweat.

"I would like to be on standby for Florence, please. Is it possible for this morning?" he asked the airline counter person at the other end of the phone.

"We can put you on a plane from Gatwick at 7:45 a.m.–this morning."

Peter groaned and looked at the clock. Insane, impossible, improbable!

"I would like to book it," he said, pulling off his pajamas and grabbing his clothes from the chair. He managed to get out his credit card and put on his socks at the same time. He pulled up his trousers and inched on his shirt while filling the kettle. He wrote a quick note to the children while he quoted his credit card information to the sleepy person working nights at a booking office.

He called a taxi. The night shift driver was a drowsy buddy he knew well from school.

"Step on it," said Peter, mimicking an American accent. This challenge was enough to wake up his friend, and off they sped towards the airport.

An early flight might have the advantage of fewer people getting on, and Peter just made it onto the plane before takeoff.

A small smile crept across his face as he crossed off his first big hurdle. No more drama. He would arrive in Florence later this very morning, and he would be discrete, invisible, a perfect tourist, and his best detective self. He was glad he didn't dress like Sherlock Holmes, but inside he was still that man, eyes drinking in the details of dust in corners, worn heels on shoes, earphones for music, even the breath of a guard.

Michael just could not have done this!

The minute Peter arrived in Florence, he phoned Michael on his mobile phone.

"Dad?" he asked his phone.

"Having a lovely time, thank you!"

"I'm here in Italy!" Peter said.

"You're what? Bad line. Breaking up!"

"I'm here in Florence!"

"In Florence?"

"I'm coming to see you now."

"It's our anniversary, Peter! Bad timing!"

"I'm on my way. Put the kettle on!"

"Peter. Why are you here?"

"I'll be pulling up outside your hotel in five minutes!"

"Oh, bloody hell!"

Peter rang off, stuffed his phone into his pocket, and smiled. If Michael was annoyed, it meant he still might have the cups. Peter smiled, imagining his father hunting for a hiding place.

Peter paid the taxi driver and dashed into the hotel.

"Michael Evans, please," he said to the manager.

"I'm afraid they have just checked out," said the Italian manager.

"Sorry, what?" Peter stammered.

"They just left with their suitcases."

Peter groaned. His suspicions were satisfied. He was sure he now knew the real thieves.

THE CHASE

Peter rushed outside. Where were they? He cocked his head. Not a sound, no puffing or panting. Did they actually go this way? Did they get a taxi or just run for it? He thought he saw someone run around that corner. Peter ran towards the dark corner. They were gone. He listened once more. He thought he heard someone breathing and looked behind him.

"Dad?" shouted Peter. "Come out! I know you're there!"

A horse clip-clopped past, pulling a cart full of eggplants, peas, carrots, and lettuce. He had lost them.

Were they on their way back to England now? Would they be caught? Peter was extremely reluctant to report them–his real father and his own mother. Hadn't they just found themselves as a family, for heaven's sake? He could not bring himself to make the call. He had hoped he could have confronted them quietly on the train. He'd have to cancel his reservation home on the plane at some point, somehow.

Peter imagined how he, Peter, would have dropped the silver cups at a police station and dashed away, with nobody the wiser. He loved his parents. He was furious at them! How could they do this, especially Angela, so sober and sensible as a mother? Peter imagined her weaving secrets into her sewing, like the women with their knitting histories in Dickens' *A Tale of Two Cities*.

Peter stopped back at the hotel.

"I thought they told the taxi driver they were going to Paris to get the train to England," said the concierge.

"Taxi driver? Train?" Peter swore under his breath. He thought of his return flight to Gatwick. It couldn't be helped. He waved at a taxi, jumped in, and headed for the train station.

Michael couldn't be far. Peter knew him well enough. Now a middle-aged man, but still a brisk walker, he was hardly the runner he had been in his younger days, so he would naturally have to get to the Florence train station by taxi. Since the Chunnel had opened, it was now a fairly quick and easy getaway from Italy to Paris and then to England. Peter looked at his watch. They must only be about fifteen minutes ahead of him.

Peter's ears absorbed the meaning of the news. The cups were still missing. Airport security high: dogs, *chiens!* Train stations on alert, but much safer for a getaway!

Michael would be caught and would die in a French prison on Elba Island. Peter would have to move to France just to visit him regularly in prison. Peter's detective mind began to open wide to the possibilities. One possibility nagging him was the fact that his father could not be the thief. Wasn't Angela having hip pains again? How could she run or even walk quickly? Then Peter remembered the wheelchairs in the airport, how those people were whisked through all the barriers and queues with a nod and a smile. But surely, they—a conventional middle-aged couple—could not be suspected? Who needed extra excitement at that age? Maybe his father? He would surely die in jail! Did train stations now have wheelchairs?

There was nothing left to do but to get to Paris and take the Chunnel back through Dover and London, perhaps spotting Michael and Angela, but recovering finally at home in Rottingdean.

Peter hailed a passing taxi and gave the taxi driver an encouragingly large note and got to the Florence train station, running onto the platform just in time to see Michael and Angela managing to get on the train. He leapt into the last car's closing doors just before the train pulled out.

FOILED

Peter sat down in a plush First-Class seat to catch his breath. He left enough time to pass so that Michael and Angela could find their seats, settle in, and feel safe. Then he worked his way along the train, checking compartments and seats, as the Italian Alps turned into the rolling hills and vineyards of France.

He was nearing the other end of the train without a hint of their existence.

"Scusi," he tried.

The conductor smiled. "Oui?"

"Ah! French now."

"I can speak English," the conductor added with a strong accent and a click of his heels.

"Ah," Peter said again. "Is there any chance you might have seen a middle-aged couple from England getting on this train?"

Peter felt it was hopeless, but he had learned to ask obvious questions, as nothing was ever as he thought it should have been.

"Yes, indeed," said the conductor.

Peter started with a smile.

The conductor added, "They got off the train at the last station."

"They what?" said Peter, turning and dashing to the door which had just closed. The train whistled through the green, lush countryside and Peter's parents had tested his patience more than any of his children had ever done.

They were making their getaway as he fumed. Had they spotted him? He pulled out his mobile phone to check anything that might make the time disappear: each second they were further away. Peter felt his heart and told himself to take a breath and use this moment to gather information and make a plan.

The train pulled into the next station, and Peter jumped off. Best idea was to wait for the next train at the very front of it, so they would not see him if they were indeed on it.

That last stop where they alighted was in the middle of bloody nowhere. Peter surmised that their only hope was to get the next train. After half-an-hour Peter watched another train going to Paris pull into the quaint station and saw that nobody got off. He got on and sat down, slinking into a soft seat in a car with several busy people in it. He looked at his watch. Three hours to go. He would stay put until they got off.

Peter almost fell asleep thinking about his children. He awoke with a jolt and saw that the train was in Paris and had already stopped. He leapt up and out in time to see his father and mother further down the crowded platform, pulling two small rolling suitcases, and Michael carrying a suspicious backpack that he always said he would never carry. And then they disappeared into a taxi.

"La Gare du Nord!" Peter almost yelled. "Vite, s'il vous plait!" he added.

"Monsieur," said the taxi driver, who, with his goatee, nodded, but couldn't hurry one bit, as the traffic was at a standstill. No point in hurrying. The driver took a drag from his Gaulois cigarette and turned up the radio. It was that lovely song, "Milord," sung by Edith Piaf.

The taxi soon wove expertly through the slow traffic and then turned sharply down a narrow brick lane meant only for bicycles and pedestrians. The driver's little mustached smile hinted at his plan, and an abrupt turn down another narrow lane gave Peter a sense that he might even overtake his father's taxi.

Peter felt exhausted, but he also knew he had a good chance of intercepting his parents. He glanced at his watch. Peter prided himself on his exact memory of train departures and arrivals for the Chunnel. This hobby went back to his boyhood love of train schedules. It was like breathing. Excitement came when the Chunnel had opened, and Peter casually memorized the new times. Wasn't there a train leaving in a quarter of an hour?

"Merci!" Peter said, waving the note back at the taxi driver, who blew more smoke and nodded his amused smile.

Peter's imagination grew riotous as he pushed his way through the throngs of multi-colored faces at la Gare du Nord. There were two trains he could catch. An earlier one he could make or the next one. If they were there, they would probably only make the later train.

Peter decided to take the second train. He bought a ticket and went to the waiting area. Loudspeakers announced arrivals and departures in French that were hard to understand, and English, which were muffled, but he picked up the word London along the way. The information signs confirmed it.

People were entering the train going to England, pushy and hurried, pulling cases and backpacks heavy upon their backs; children crying, the Brits queuing, the French and Italians pushing to get a seat. If the Brits were irate, they kept their thoughts to themselves, except for one passenger.

"'Ere, mate! Me wife was standing 'ere before you. That's 'er seat an all!"

"Pardonnez-moi!" said a polite, if hurried, Frenchman, who then stood up for the other man's wife.

How civilized, thought Peter.

Peter looked at his watch. The doors were closing. Last-minute passengers were squeezing in through the closing doors. Peter looked up to see Angela and Michael pushing through the closing doors down the platform. Peter jumped up and made a dash for it, and just managed to squeeze through the doors near him.

Michael and Angela were three cars further down the train from him. He wasn't sure if they had seen him. Their gleeful faces could have been from pure joy at escaping with the cups. Peter couldn't believe these two people were his very own parents, and he was a detective on their scent.

He picked up a section of *Le Figaro,* which was lying on a seat in his car, folded it, and began to make his way through the carriages. He had an hour and a half to get there, so he sat in each car, making his way closer to them with each move, while they were in the Chunnel where they could not alight. He planned his maneuvers carefully. He knew both of them would be exhausted by now, and at least one might nod off. They would be hoarding the cups like koala bears, so he would have to distract the one who was holding them, most likely Michael.

Peter was sweating. If he succeeded, he would have to get away from them immediately and probably they would never talk to him again. He had to risk it. Otherwise, they would go to jail–both of them. It was an impossible thought. Their spirits would wither in there. They would sink away into depression and finally die right there. Peter had to save them. He feared he would lose his job as a police detective forever if he were found out.

He glanced at the next set of interior doors he would finally pass through to the final compartment. He stood and wished for a moment he had not brought his case. The cups would never fit into it.

The glass doors between the two carriages shielded him from the next one, where he spotted Angela and Michael sitting facing each other. His mother was obviously nodding off. He couldn't tell about Michael, whose back was to him. Peter opened the doors, unfolded his newspaper, and inched towards them. He sat behind Michael. Surely that was a snort from Michael. He was also asleep!

Peter became alert, as he knew the train was just about to arrive at the first stop in England. He would have to work quickly. He could hardly breathe. It had to work. The train was slowing down. The green fields and trees informed him it was now or never. The train was coming to a gentle stop. Peter lifted Michael's heavy arm like it was a feather, sliding the small backpack from under Michael's arm along the seat. Peter put his own bag in its place and lowered Michael's arm and tucked Michael's backpack under his own arm, got up, and with a stealth practiced since his childhood detective adventures, moved into the next carriage, ready to make a dash at the next stop. People kept reading or dozing off.

It wasn't going to be easy. No, he knew that. But it had to be done. When he thought of his past endeavors, he actually felt angry, but mostly at himself. He could almost growl deep down. In fact, he noticed he was actually growling. A woman on the train looked nervously at him and shifted in her seat, unobtrusively and politely. He smiled at her and mumbled, "Sorry!" She nodded but looked away, out the window at the sheep and cows, and little villages, each larger than the last.

OUTWITTED

Peter's nerves were definitely frayed. He couldn't resist. The train stopped at a station. He got off and took Michael's backpack into the toilet and opened it.

"What?"

He looked at the porcelain cups in the package and swore.

"Porcelain?" he almost yelled.

Michael had outwitted him. He had been sure that Michael had the silver cups. Peter had been determined to get them and return them to Italy, where they belonged. Peter felt an urgency, based on his belief that bad luck, indeed, came to those who owned them until they were housed in Cellini's own country.

Peter hurriedly got back on the train and edged over to Michael, who was snoring, and gently pulled his own bag from under Michael's arm, slipping the backpack containing the porcelain cups back where it had been. Then he worked his way back to his seat three cars ahead and sat down, glancing at the woman as he controlled a new growling sound. He castigated himself for his lack of self-control and watched as she pointedly searched the scenery and then her handbag.

Was there something familiar about her? He couldn't put his finger on exactly what it was. Perhaps the way she pretended not to be interested.

Perhaps it was how she got up and moved to another seat further away, in such a way that she could, perhaps, see him better. He brushed his discomfort off, but then he remembered that all his life, his feelings had come, not just out of the blue, but in relation to something that was really going on. He was not psychic–he was observant from habit. But a lot of it was unconscious and mostly he didn't feel the need to follow his instinct when a case was not involved. No–he was just being his usual suspicious self–a great way for a detective to be. Poor woman–suspected–yet quite innocent. He stored it in his inner bank of suspicious, yet blameless, characters. Now she did not look familiar at all.

The train screeched to a halt in between two stations. Everybody looked up at the same time. Could be a cow on the tracks. Peter's ears and eyes fell into his detective mode. Nothing out of either window gave a hint of a problem. The glass doors between the next car and his car opened and a large man with a black hat and beady, dark eyes scanned the compartment. The woman ducked behind a newspaper. The train started moving again.

Peter pretended to read his own paper. The man sat down right next to Peter. Alarmed, Peter scrunched nearer to the window. The man's broad shoulders brushed his own.

Peter felt this stranger was not from England. He smelled like what? This man was surely Italian–a scent of garlic, perhaps? Peter started sweating despite the cool weather. He dared not look. His eyes studied his newspaper while he imagined himself leaping up and jumping off the moving train. Then he imagined he was just losing his mind! The man had a right to smell like garlic! What was he thinking? He now suspected everyone!

When they arrived in St. Pancras in London, Peter darted off the train onto the platform. He couldn't help wondering if these strangers were the police or the mafia. If they were the police, he might have exchanged a civil comment in normal circumstances. But now he was on the wrong side.

Peter realized that, perhaps, now, he did not really have to protect his parents, who would soon be pacing their way along the platform, along with a bustling crowd of hurrying passengers weaving past them.

As he pushed down the platform well ahead of them, he wondered if he should take a side trip, and briefly stop by his office in London, or if it would be best to go straight to Rottingdean to his house, and then to Angela and Michael's house to see them after they had also returned. He was exhausted and didn't feel like being convivial at the office.

After he bought a ticket from St. Pancras to Brighton, Peter aimed his tired body, along with the crowd on the platform, towards his train to Brighton, just in time to rush on to the train before it pulled south out of the station.

His parents had quite fooled him. This time, he figured they would be on the next train after his. But he now knew that they didn't have the silver cups. Peter was tired and needed to think. He settled into his seat on the train and stared out the window at the endless backs of buildings with their bricked-up windows, dating back to 1850. The view eventually evaporated into sprinkles of green hills and cows. As the train flew south, he glanced at the old, quaint villages that had hardly changed in centuries. One day he might stop at one of them and see what had quietly held them together like glue–but not today. He closed his eyes and began to nod off, thinking about his children and Susan.

An hour later he got out at the Brighton train station, its population getting on with their day: quiet, polite, and reasonably sober. He hailed a taxi to his home in Rottingdean, another village that had hardly changed in centuries.

He got out and paid the driver, another old friend from their school days.

"Cheerio, Peter!" said his friend.

"Cheerio, then! Ta," said Peter, paying his fare, and turning to go into his house.

INDEPENDENT NATURES

Peter walked in the front door, pulled his fingers through his rather long hair, went upstairs, and emptied the contents of his bag onto his bed, came down, and made a nice hot cup of tea.

Then Peter phoned his parents at their home, but no one answered. They would be home soon enough. He liked to start a case, even if it was about his parents, with his goal. It seemed to save time, rather than putting one foot in front of the other and working more by instinct. Of course, he would never call it instinct to his workmates—instinct was still too feminine to admit to. But he knew it was what he did. The other side of him, the logical side, insisted on a plan, starting at the goal and working backwards.

He relaxed as he drank his tea, and the confusion of his life sank away. It fought with another of his goals. They battled around his skull until one won—he was going to save his parents from themselves. His own dear children, for once, had to take a back seat. Now, working backwards from this goal, what was next?

Peter felt that his parents were now moving into a new stage of life—there was no doubt about it. They were frequently rebelling, giggling, and frowning at whatever they felt like. Who cared who was looking?

Michael was evidently still trying to run despite his usual arthritic complaints. He said he now ran more slowly and often walked quickly as an alternative. But he was fairly fit for his age. Angela was slowing down but walked behind Michael every day to "keep her health" until he met her on the way back from his run. In spite of the rebellion, giggling, and frowning, her mind was perfect. She put it down to her quilting, which she also managed to keep doing almost every day.

Peter couldn't help it—he drove over to their house. He decided to knock at their door, although he knew they never locked it, and he knew they always said he could just go in. But he held back until he heard one of them yell, as usual, "Come in, Peter!"

Peter walked into the kitchen and sat down, as usual. "How was your trip, then?" he ventured.

His parents smiled at each other.

"Fine, Peter," said Michael, crunching his English muffin topped with strawberry jam and clotted cream. "A bit of a runaround in the end, almost missing trains and altogether too much running. I think someone nicked my bag of toiletries right as we stopped in England this side of the Chunnel. I am not sure—perhaps just my imagination. But when I looked again, it was back under my arm. I must have been dreaming. Very strange! What happened to you, then?"

Peter dared not meet their eyes. "I was really calling from England," he lied. He studied his fingernails. Maybe they didn't realize he was the one.

"Here's a cup of tea, love," said Angela.

"How do you like our new porcelain cups?" added Michael.

"Very nice," said Peter, raising an eyebrow.

"Right, then!" said Michael. "Did you see the news?" Michael seemed to smile in a subtle way as he passed the newspaper to Peter.

Peter read the article: CELLINI CUPS FOUND!

"Well, that's a relief!" said Peter, digging deeper into the article, pretending to be surprised. Of course, he had already seen the paper. But he didn't want them to think he'd visited them because of it.

"It appears they were found in a loo at the Gare du Nord train station. Some boy found them—an English boy."

"Did he get a reward?" asked Angela.

Peter checked the end of the article.

"No. They didn't say so here," Peter said. "I think he should, don't you?"

Angela poured more tea and offered Peter a muffin.

"Wasn't that about the same time we were there?" asked Angela, looking as innocent as her name.

"Yes," said Michael.

"Italy is a beautiful country," Peter said, sipping his tea.

"Indeed, indeed!" said Michael, taking a large bite out of his muffin.

"I'd love to go there again," said Angela.

Peter looked up nervously, a pleasant smile hiding his extreme horror at this possibility of future trouble with them. *Don't ever go there again. I am getting way too old for all this!*

THE SUNSET–1930

Sir Frederick didn't care if Conor didn't talk for days. It suited him as he pondered his millions under the floorboards. He rode high behind the large steering wheel and kept his eyes on the weather that he was approaching, as well as taking a cursory scan of the size of the white-caps around his boat. The wind was perfect, and he sailed his yacht, slicing the small waves like he owned them. Conor was nipping along the bow, checking the sails.

"You hungry, mate?" shouted Conor.

"I am, indeed," said Frederick. "Be sure to add beans today, fry the eggs and potatoes and add a tin of tomatoes."

"Coming up," said Conor, jumping down the hatch and into the galley below.

Conor liked to sing sea shanties, mostly Irish, and other songs about politics. Most of the time Frederick couldn't make out the words, but he liked the positive sounds and how they made him feel.

He felt sorry for all those friends back in England who'd lost their money so abruptly. Some had jumped from tall buildings just before he'd sailed. Why hadn't they listened to Frederick? He just knew there was going to be a crash. It was better to be sailing the world now than to be watching the people he knew so well falling to their knees and begging for help. After the stock market crash of 1929, Frederick had started to give his money away, but then he realized he would also go down with them if he kept it up. What else could he do? So, he packed up and left on his paid-off yacht.

Although he had Conor for company, Sir Frederick was lonely. The stars at night winked at him, reminding him of how little he mattered in the grand scheme of things. The giant waves that periodically threatened to topple the boat were clear messages about the possibility of sudden drowning. And yet, the sunsets were spectacular and seemed worth it all. Even the beautiful bulbous clouds marching towards his yacht from behind, promising a storm, reminded him of his very unimportant self. He laughed to think of capsizing with all that gold going down to the bottom of the sea, perhaps never to be found.

"Breakfast's ready," said Conor from the galley. He lifted up a tray containing a steaming hot meal through the hatch. Frederick set it by his side and rode the waves as he warmed his insides.

He hardly thought of his ex-wife now. The moment was everything. His heading and safety were all that really mattered. Conor was a boon— a true sailor and a great cook. He polished everything on the boat until it was sparkling.

Sir Frederick had finally arrived at the hundreds of islands of the South Pacific, stopping at several of them along the way to get fresh fruit and eggs and nameless, strange delicacies not yet known by him. He was heading towards the myriad islands on the way to Suva, the main Fijian island in the South Pacific. He looked forward to drinking more coconut juice. He finished off his breakfast and handed the tray down to Conor. A second hot cup of coffee was passed up to him and life, just at that delightful moment, was so very fine.

Conor came up to join him with a cup of coffee.

And then, there it was—that other possibility he had always feared— the moment which all sailors feared, yet felt it was worth the risk. A huge and ear-crushing bump under his sailboat that lifted the whole boat out of the water and slammed it sideways. Frederick was clipped to the boat, as usual.

"Help!" yelled Conor as he was propelled overboard.

Again, the whale surfaced and lifted the boat completely out of the water. Warm blood oozed from Frederick's head. Before his final breath, he saw a flash of the yellow and orange sunset at the horizon. His hands flayed outwards. A final bump by the whale forced the salty ocean water into the drowning boat as it plunged downwards into the deep. Sir Frederick's lungs filled with water, and he blacked out—forever.

The whale swam away towards the sunset. The boat was, indeed, sinking to the bottom of the sea.

PAINS

Over the following weeks, Susan seemed to be very preoccupied and after a while, Peter decided not to pursue her unless she contacted him. She could linger alone in her busy life for a long time. Peter had his own preoccupations to attend to—especially for his children—who were possibly still haunted by the suspicion that he had pushed Jeannie to her death. He knew they loved him, and they knew Jeannie, in some of her wilder moments, was capable of jumping.

Peter picked up his penny whistle and played an Irish tune slowly. He envisioned an Irish funeral, the drums, the green jackets and shirts, the casket, and the solemn faces of a thousand generations. It was a glance of Jeannie, some streak of her Irish ancestors, and he played his whistle like he was the physicality of their souls.

"Dad," said Cassandra, coming down from her room.

"Oh!" Peter said, stopping abruptly.

"That was lovely. You never play!"

He put his whistle down and turned back into her father and not a grieving widower. How many years would this go on?

"My love," he started. "Feeling a bit lonely for your mother, if you must know the truth."

"You can play it anyway, Dad. Mom can hear you–somehow. Maybe she's right here, floating around, pleased that we are speaking about her and very pleased to hear your heavenly song to her."

"Well, maybe so, Cassandra. But what are you doing home from school?" Peter walked towards her and noticed her eyes were red.

"Got my period, that's all."

"Oh, right," Peter said, trying to look like a modern single father. But still, that part of things was a woman's world to him, and there before him stood the evidence, wiping her cheeks delicately. At least she didn't get angry like Jeannie had done.

"Pains?" he asked, with no mother to help the girl along.

"Terrible, Dad. I just couldn't sit there in agony, slumped over my desk, holding back the moans that came from my mouth whether or not I wanted them to."

She looked at him in a pleading way that took him back to her first period, when he was the only parent she had to tell.

"Come here, my love," he said, opening his arms. Cassandra shuffled over and let herself be embraced.

"Now, my love," he said after a quiet hug, "Get back in bed, and I'll bring you a nice hot cup of tea!"

Cassandra smiled, kissed his cheek, and skated back up to her room in her slippers, making slapping sounds as she went.

Peter put the kettle on and while it boiled, he picked up his penny-whistle and played "Mrs. McGraff." He could almost imagine Jeannie back when she was Cassandra's age, doing a jig around the kitchen. He wondered about Jeannie–were they happy then? Weren't they in love? Indeed, they were. Indeed, there was passion, mostly ignited by an imp-ish young lady who had not been burdened down yet by three children and Peter's flimsy income.

Peter thought he'd better have a talk with Cassandra soon, before she ended up like Jeannie. There was a women's clinic opening up in Rottingdean. He would make an appointment through his doctor. That was the least he could do. There were terrors like AIDS he feared for her. She might not marry young like he and Jeannie had. She needed to know about condoms and how some boys were after her for less than a marriage certificate. Of course, most likely, she already knew all that by now!

He lifted the whistling teakettle off the gas flame and made an old-fashioned small pot of tea, put it on the tray with a few sweet biscuits, and carried it up into his darling daughter's bedroom.

"Oh, Daddy! Thank you!" she sobbed, turning into the pillow, her shoulders shaking. Peter stood still, tray in hand. Was there something she wasn't telling him about? At least she was not pregnant!

It was strange how a parent and a child could bond over a pot of tea. Here they sat, now, Cassandra drying her tears, sipping tea from her special teacup, and Peter pouring his own and adding one spoonful of sugar, and then a bit.

"What's going on, my love?" he said.

"Oh, Daddy, it's Mum. I loved her so much. I miss her so…."

At the risk of spilling his tea and knocking over hers, he leaned over and put his open hand under her wet chin and said, "How I miss our Mum, too!" Secretly, he was relieved to hear Cassandra was not pregnant!

"Will it ever end, this sadness, Dad?"

"It will soften as time goes by, but no, it will never end. We only get one mother."

"Dad?"

"Yes, my love?"

"You won't die for a long time, right?"

He took her hand. "I will never die!"

"Dad! I'm serious!"

"Well, I plan to be at your graduation and beyond, so not to worry about me!"

"Promise?"

"Promise! Now drink up and let's get a move on with the morning!" He knocked back the dregs and stood up, brushing the non-existent crumbs from his trousers.

"One thing, Dad…."

He sat back down. Maybe she was pregnant and really needed to talk to someone.

"I'm not pregnant, but I've missed my periods."

"What? But you said…have you been…?"

"Not possibly pregnant, Dad!"

"Okay. I'll make an appointment with Doctor Parker right away, just to be sure…."

"I am NOT pregnant!"

"Only one way to know that!"

"Dad, you need a father or at least…sperm…to get pregnant!"

"Right. Not a problem then," he said, a lingering question lurking in his eyes. Peter turned and went towards the door, then turned back.

"Dad! Not a chance!"

"You wouldn't be frightened to tell me if something like that–who knows what–were to happen to you, would you?"

"Go away, Dad. I'm getting up."

Peter went back to her bed, picked up the tray with the teacups and teapot on it, and bowed.

"Me Lady!" he said, exiting backwards like a butler.

PATTERN

As per Dr. Parker's suggestion, Peter arranged for Cassandra to start therapy with Helen.

A few days later, Peter waited nervously for Cassandra in Helen's waiting room. He searched Cassandra's smooth face when she came out of Helen's office.

"Stop worrying, Dad! Let's go!"

Peter stood up and prepared to go. Helen came out, and they shook hands.

"It's been a while," Helen said.

"Too long!" Peter said.

"See you next week, then," she said, looking at Cassandra.

Peter and Cassandra left arm-in-arm, and Peter suggested that they drop by the pub to talk in the garden.

Cassandra had a tomato juice and Peter stuck to half a pint of beer. The sun was still just out, but the shadows were long. They talked about the nice warm weather and Peter finally asked how it went.

"She's nice," said Cassandra. "She smiles too much. It's just American, isn't it? It feels nice until you remember they all smile that way."

Peter remembered how uncomfortable Helen's smile had made him at first. Then he got used to it. He expected it. In fact, he would later have thought something was wrong if she didn't smile that way.

"She has a lovely smile and I do agree, it's an American habit."

"I suppose everybody must be that much happier in the USA, always smiling. Don't they ever have troubles?"

"I'll bet even our therapist has had troubles, or how would she even be able to help us out?"

"That's a point, Dad. Of course, I don't have any troubles. But you and Mum did, so I'm left to sort them out. Doesn't seem fair!"

"Everybody has secret wonderings, Cassandra, especially the normal-looking people. Think of your friends at school. Who looks happy and normal? Now, what secrets do they harbor?"

"Oh, Dad, that's exaggerating. Or that's so American!"

"Must have learned it from our therapist!"

They smiled, as if they shared a big secret.

It began to rain.

"Couldn't the sun just stay there for a couple of hours?" moaned Cassandra.

"It seems to love to rain at night around here. But here it comes!"

Cassandra pulled her small, fold-up umbrella out of her rucksack, and they got up and strode back inside through the garden entrance. Then she closed her umbrella and waded through the customers sensibly sitting inside. Cassandra and Peter made their way out of the main entrance towards home, with a feeling of warmth and camaraderie surrounding the sprinkles that threatened to turn into a storm.

The next week, as Peter drove to Helen's office to drop Cassandra off, he mulled over his situation. He realized that he thought rather too much about Helen. She had always been attractive to him, but he had been so distraught about Jeannie, there had been no way he could have considered her in any other than a professional manner. But now, several years older and wiser on both sides, he couldn't help thinking of her differently. A relationship with her would be unprofessional, of course.

"Hello!" he said in a jolly, smiling, perhaps too friendly manner as Helen opened the door. He glanced at her ring finger. It was bare of official commitment. Peter peered at the skin on his left ring finger and realized there was no indication at all that he once wore a wedding ring.

Helen was now more British than American. She smiled, lowering her eyes, and beckoned Cassandra into her office.

"Dad, I can walk home," said Cassandra, turning her head in a way that swung her hair out, but in a way that alerted Peter that he might be caught. "You don't have to wait!"

Daughters, he mused, miss nothing.

SECRETIVE

When Cassandra left the house the next day, Peter admitted to himself that she, now seventeen, was blossoming into a tall, graceful, and wise version of her mother.

Peter felt proud of his daughter–proud and concerned for her welfare. He wondered if all parents feared for their children as he did. Or, now that he thought about it, he feared more for her than he did the boys. So far, they had not been interested in anything more dangerous than cricket.

Cassandra, on the other hand, was secretive. After their discussion about her non-existent periods and her visits to Helen, she had stopped her usual chattering–at least with him. He guessed it was because now she had a woman she could confide in.

Peter felt his heart flutter in Helen's presence, but while Cassandra was her client, he realized Helen had to be professional, leaving him with a courteous smile and a comforting arm around Cassandra's shoulders. But still, he was Cassandra's only parent, and Cassandra's silences unnerved him lately.

Something bothered Peter about this new quiet at home. Sometimes he felt Jeannie's presence. He felt the gravity of this house's history weighing heavily on his shoulders: the stabbed cat, the lurking midnight moments of his mentally diminishing wife and the arguments. A fond memory surfaced, as he remembered the children when they were young and wanted to sit on his lap.

Peter got up and went to the kitchen window, shifted a pan into the drainer, wiped his hands on the dishtowel, and stretched his imagination across the ocean to Italy.

"Cellini," he said aloud, "Can you still be haunting us?"

Why was Cassandra so quiet these days? He told himself to let her go. She was almost grown up. Let her be. Be supportive, but not nosy. He relied completely on Helen. Thank goodness he trusted Helen. But actually, he realized, Helen knew everything about him, and he knew hardly anything about her.

He picked up the phone and called her.

COFFEE SHOP

Peter walked down the hill to meet Helen at the coffee shop. She had said it would be fine, as long as it was "just friends." She was on a break. Her eyes were sparkling, like an innocent doe. She always looked young and energetic to Peter, and rather serious when she looked directly into his eyes. The look was that of an untarnished child, unencumbered by layers of history, expecting the truth, the good, the possible. Peter had seen too much in his life by now to believe a person his age could still be an optimist. Imagine all the secrets Helen must carry around about people's health problems, fears of unemployment, marital breakdowns, drug overdoses!

"You look happy," he ventured.

"It's the American in me, I guess," she said.

"Why are you Americans always so optimistic in the face of all the horrible things that you obviously see, just as much as we Brits do?"

"I was born that way. I had a young, musical mother, who burst into a song that she liked if she'd heard it on the radio–and anywhere–but mostly driving. She loved to sing in the car."

"Driving? So, you learned to be happy while being a child in the back seat?"

"Something like that. She also had a great British habit of saying, 'Nevermind,' when disaster struck."

"Ah! We do say that, don't we?"

"So," she said, confidentially, her wide eyes searching Peter's face. "Sorry, can't talk about Cassandra."

"I know, I know!" Peter fiddled with his ear. "Actually, it was about us."

"Us?"

"You and me," he said.

"Oh!"

"I mean...." Peter said, reaching his hands towards hers across the table.

She looked at his gesture but did not pull her hands away.

"It's awkward, Peter," she said.

"I know. It's unprofessional, for starters."

"Yes...." she said.

"Yes. In fact, it's happened to me," said Peter.

"And me," she confessed.

Peter felt like he was sitting there with no clothes on. They had gone so slowly for so many years. Could there really be hope?

"Helen!" he spluttered.

"Peter, please let me continue."

Peter looked at her face and froze.

"I'm married," she confessed.

Although Peter wanted to depart immediately, he was trained by this lovely woman to stay in the uncomfortable moment.

"I didn't realize...," he said, glancing at her bare ring finger.

"I'm sorry. He lives in California, and we rarely see each other. It is more about convenience now."

"Couldn't I make it inconvenient?"

"You are sweet, Peter. I saw this coming, but there is no way I can divorce him. He is paralyzed, in a home, but quite conscious mentally. I can't hurt him in that state. Call it brotherly love. It just isn't possible."

"I see," Peter said, sad and shocked that she was married, and sorry about her husband, but, perhaps, somewhat relieved that her husband was paralyzed and far away in California.

"What about that lovely lady you met at the airport?" she said, changing the subject.

"Oh," Peter said to his ex-therapist. "I forgot I told you about her. Damn this honest relationship! It's all your fault!"

Helen smiled. "I know you well, Peter. But don't forget, it's not an uncommon problem, this therapist and patient bit. I've heard it all. Nothing surprises me at this stage!"

"Life is very complicated!"

"You wouldn't believe how complicated it really is!"

"I would!" He gently pulled his hands away from hers and took a sip of tea.

"So, Peter," Helen said. "What's going on?"

"No therapy!" he responded.

"Sorry! Old habit!"

"Indeed. The usual. You know the stories. Much the same. Strangers in town that everybody suspects of all the bad things that have happened here for centuries."

"Plenty of strangers in the harbor all those centuries!"

"Exactly!" Peter was off. "But it's true. These people come from London and get on welfare and never even try to look for a job."

"Are there jobs here to find?"

"True," he said. "Not much choice, unless you like the smell of fish." They laughed.

"About Cassandra," he said.

"Yes," she said, raising a cautious eyebrow.

"She's acting strange. Have you noticed?"

"Professional secrecy, Peter, you know that."

Peter looked down at his empty cup. "It's just that she's stopped talking to me. She's always been so honest and forthcoming. Now, it's all sulking in her room."

"That's natural for her age—a natural separation between parent and teenager." She smiled. "How are you, I mean, besides Cassandra?"

"We can talk about that, can't we?" he asked.

"Anytime," she said.

"The weather's turned cloudy, have you noticed?"

"Yes, Peter. But seriously, how are you doing?"

Peter knew he had no choice. She knew him too well. He would have to tell her the latest about Susan.

Unbroken Rule

Some days later, after work, Helen sat across from Peter in the other soft leather chair by the pub's fire. Peter couldn't hear the noisy laughter of the darts players on the other side of the pub. All he could hear was her soft voice. All he could see were those kind eyes. He felt like falling into her arms for comfort. But, of course, she would not suspect such a thing now that he knew about her husband.

"Let me get you a drink," he offered. She looked up. The bartender was approaching with a glass of tomato juice.

"Oh! You must have influence here!" said Peter, glad to settle into the arms of his comfortable chair.

"So! How's it going?" she asked.

"Funny you should ask. I confess it isn't the peace-and-quiet I was expecting. Sometimes it is just too quiet, and other times, it is a zoo. The kids were all supposed to be off down the road living in someone else's rented rooms, while I sat listening to classical music and pouring a second cup of tea!"

"Ah!" said Helen in her sympathetic way.

"I mean it. It's rather noisy now, with everybody coming and going! I had a vision," he went on, "of living back in Hampstead and settling down with a partner." He stole a glance at her throat. Yes, she was swallowing with a little choke, and looking forward, apparently, to her tomato juice.

"I would have missed your company, Peter," she said.

"Oh, really? Well, part of me had a vision that you might want to move to London, too!" He dared not say, "with me."

"Oh, no. That is very sweet of you. But I'm very ensconced in my work here," she said. "Think of how my patients would feel–quite bereft, for sure."

"Of course, of course!" he stammered.

"I have to add," she said, kindly, "that of all my ex-patients, I would miss you the most if you moved away."

"Helen. Perhaps you could stop thinking of me as a patient or ex-patient. That was so long ago, don't you think?"

"Well, Peter, you know that there is the ethical side I must look after," she said, sipping her tea and gazing steadily at him, which made him smile and wonder if he could push the conversation a little further.

"Where does it say a therapist can't see her former patients outside the therapy room?"

"It is just a rule. Some people have paid dearly for making that mistake."

"Yes," said Peter, "but those were dirty old men preying on young girls, right?"

"Some," she said, her eyes hard on him. "It does seem archaic now, doesn't it?"

Peter looked deeply into those beautiful eyes and held his body erect, as if hoping to hear more. But she left it to him to continue.

"Well, Helen, if you ever feel that more would be possible between us, just give me a nod!" he laughed and raised his glass. She raised hers and gave a slight nod.

He knocked back half the glass and noticed a definite nod.

"Woman," he said, having liberated his tongue, "just curious, am I in the running, perhaps?"

Helen nodded again and gave him a winning smile. He was annoyed only because he realized she could read his mind.

"All right, Peter. You win," she said. "You are definitely in the running, but I shall suffer from guilt, and Freud will haunt my dreams. Shall we have a proper date next week?"

"That would be lovely!" he replied, astonished, remembering her husband. "What about going up to London?"

"Sounds perfect!" she said.

They made plans and parted with anticipatory smiles.

BRAKES

"I completely understand," said Peter the next Friday into his
phone, more angry than understanding. He gazed out the window at the
blue sky and the distant frolicking waves, and then at his overnight case,
packed and full of promise.

He carried the case back up to his bedroom and slung it on the bed.
How carefully he had added just enough clothes for only a weekend in
London. So much could have happened. And now, nothing, no plans, a
sense of emptiness he could identify that seemed like the first weeks after
Jeannie had died.

Helen was clearly a careful person. She'd had second thoughts, as was
her right. Peter knew that. One kiss and they would be on that roller-
coaster that goes way too fast, too high and too far, with no discernible
brakes. She was wise. And yet, surely, she was as ready as he was? Surely,
she needed his arm around her as much as he needed her face to nuzzle
in his neck.

She had taught him one thing, at least, when he was in therapy with
her, and that was the phrase that now rang in his ears: *she has her own
agenda.*

Of course, it had been Jeannie's agenda when she first mentioned it.
And now, ironically, it was Helen's agenda.

Of course, a cup of tea might heal everything. But instead, he dialed Susan's number like a robot. He needed comfort, and the men at the pub were not going to compensate for his disappointment.

"Hello!" he said heartily.

"Peter!" Susan said. "It's been a while!"

"I'm sorry, yes, it has. I was wondering how life's been treating you?"

Susan didn't answer at once. Peter heard the silence. He wondered how else he could have better begun the conversation.

"I told you my son was sick, didn't I? You know, all that business about epilepsy? Well, it is much, much worse, and now I think he is dying," she said in a whisper.

"Oh, Susan! I'm so sorry! Is there anything I can do to help you? Anything! I'm so very sorry!" Peter felt like a fool. It all started with the plane crash. It wasn't anything to do with Peter and yet, he had been the witness to her own reaction to the crash, and they had shared the fear for the worst for their children. Peter's were thriving. Susan's son was dying.

Life was just not fair. Death chose its victims, and there was no choice for them, or the ones left behind.

"Well, now that you ask, Peter, I could really use someone to hold my hand through this. In truth, I'm afraid I am really falling apart! Sorry!"

"Yes, yes! Just tell me. When and where?"

"Now, Peter. Could you please come to my house?"

"Of course, of course! I'll be right there–leaving this moment."

Peter left the house swiftly; happy he was still in Rottingdean to be there for Susan and her son. He leapt into the car and drove down the hill and around the shoreline towards her house with concentrated determination–and perhaps a little too quickly–to a woman who needed him.

SUSAN'S SON

Peter had not driven that quickly for years. He stood at Susan's door, panting, and reached for the bell. There was none. He grabbed the knocker and tapped it gently. Loud noises might upset Susan even more.

Peter saw a woman with red eyes and a red nose opening the door, clutching her handkerchief like it might save her from her grief. He couldn't help himself. He had been there with Jeannie. He let Susan take his coat, and then he put his arms around her.

"I am so very sorry, Susan. This is just too much. What can I do?"

"Peter," she said, backing away gently and blowing her nose. Then she stood there, small, helpless, quiet, lower lip quivering.

Peter thought she looked a mess—yet wonderful. Here she stood, almost naked in her openness with him. Her eyes searched his, and he answered by reaching his arms towards her again. She stepped forward, and, as he put his arms around her, she laid her head on his shoulder.

"Oh, Peter! I am going to die myself. I just cannot bear this!"

"Susan," he said. He held her close and kissed her wet cheek. He really didn't know what to say. Hugging her was the best he could manage. He wanted to see her son, but he found himself in this first embrace more meaning that he'd had in years, and he felt comforted. He didn't want to let her go. It was a precious moment.

Finally, she backed away, looked down, and sniffled.

"Come," she beckoned. She led him down the hallway, and they entered her son's bedroom. An elderly woman was sitting on the other side of Winston's bed.

"Oh, Peter, this is my mother," Susan said. Her mother glanced up with a nod, then leaned back in–watching–perhaps praying.

Peter decided just to nod to her, while he began to understand the horror of the moment.

Winston lay there, his face pale white, eyes closed, moving towards somewhere only he knew about.

Susan leaned over her son. "Mummy's right here, my dear darling love," she said faintly.

"Is that Peter?" Winston asked.

"Yes, he came to say hello," she said.

"You mean, 'goodbye,'" Winston whispered.

"You will get better," she said.

"Mum. Don't lie. I know I'm dying," he coughed. "I can hardly...."

Peter stood by for a minute, then it was as if he were guided to move closer and sit down by the dying teenager. Gently, he took Winston's hand and pressed his own warmth into it. Peter's eyes were soft yet glued to Winston's ghostly face. Peter began to rub Winston's hand as he had done so many times with his own children when they were ill. He had always managed to bring them round, and he tried it now, with all his being surging with parental empathy.

Susan hovered over his shoulder, holding her breath and lightly touching Peter's arm. Peter felt a pulse of power through his body that seemed to pour through his own fingers.

"Mummy," said Winston's weak voice, "Can I have some water, please?".

Susan scuttled into the bathroom with his bedside glass, filled it up and returned, holding out the glass as if it were a healing potion. Peter took the glass, lifted the boy's head slightly and helped him take the smallest sip from the straw.

When he laid his head back on the pillow, Winston's face seemed to relax, like all tension had ceased. He didn't move. His eyes closed. He had the tiniest smile. Did his chest stop moving? The three of them just stared at the dying boy, unable at first to understand that their momentary hopes might be evaporating into the warm air.

Then Susan fell across his body, crying, "You can't die, wake up, wake up!"

Peter moved his hand from Winston's hand to Susan's shoulder and he left it there, like an angel, to help her connect with life, as she held on to her son's approaching death, and prayed for a reversal of the impossible.

Peter felt his tears wash down his cheeks. He reached over to the child's grandmother and touched her shoulder for a moment. Her face was covered with a handkerchief, as muted sounds of sorrow came from behind it.

Winston moved his lips. They leaned over him, listening to his dying words.

"I love you, Mum…," he whispered, his eyes trained on Susan. And then there were gurgling sounds.

Susan looked at Peter for help. There was no help to be given. He took Susan's hand, and they watched as the life of her son slowly diminished with his last futile attempts to breathe one final breath.

"No! No! No! Winston! You cannot die! You cannot die!" she cried, resting her cheek upon his. The summer air was thick with disbelief. And then the silence in the room was as loud as thunder.

NOW

Peter hugged Susan with all his power and heart as she buried her face in his shoulder. Neither of them was willing to let go. When they did, she turned and remained by his side. His arm circled her waist, and they gazed down at Winston and his grandmother kissing Winston's forehead.

Peter remembered Jeannie's last moments and the sense of shock and relief that it was over, followed by guilt. He knew that it was normal. But guilt was still there, no matter how much he knew about it. Could Susan be going through this now?

"He was a lovely young man," said Peter.

"Was? *Was?*" spluttered Susan, who sat by Winston, laying her hand on his forehead. She waited, and looked at her mother, then sat back again, and choked out the word, "was."

Again, Susan flung her body onto Winston's, as if her warmth would awaken him, and yelled, "No, no, no! You must wake up now, Winston! Wake up!" And her tears flowed over his sheet and seeped onto his unmoving chest. Peter stood by Susan and her mother, putting his hand warmly onto her mother's shoulder—once again—just for a moment. It came too close. That brief touch revived his own terrible sorrow.

How much sadness could a person take? He had to go home and function—make tea, help the kids who swore they didn't need his help anymore. But he knew. He knew his warm body in their presence would be the help they needed. There were no words necessary. The kids only knew Winston from back when Jeannie was alive, but now he was just sixteen. The young don't die, damn it all! Only old people die and wither away.

When Peter got to her front door to leave, he opened his arms, and she fell into them. It was a long moment—yet—so short. As he walked towards his car, he glanced back at Susan's dejected figure, and mouthed a solemn, "Goodbye."

"How's Susan?" Cassandra asked Peter when he got home.

"She's a mess, of course. She's with her mum. It's really quite unbelievable. I am so sorry to tell you that Winston has died."

"Oh, my God! Ever so sorry, Dad," said Cassandra. "He was nice." She took out her handkerchief, looked away, and blew her nose.

Apart from saying, "Sorry, Dad," Henry and Oliver kept their faces buried in their respective books. But Peter knew they were a hundred percent present, just being brave. Inside, they surely were quietly crying.

Peter busied himself making tea. They finally sat down, he sipped his tea, and ate his biscuits, hardly tasting them.

The phone rang several hours later. Peter picked it up.

"Hello, Peter. It's Susan. I just wanted to thank you for being there today for me. I really fell apart, didn't I?"

"Very natural," said Peter. "Please, no apologies necessary. You're his mum! It's amazing you're able to phone me at all."

"Well, it's good to be able to share all this with you, Peter. I just wanted to thank you for your understanding ways."

Peter remembered the hug. It was an unencumbered hug, a kind that he only remembered from Jeannie when they realized they were in love. Too short—too short, that hug—that hug. Peter felt a longing deep down inside his body for just one more hug like that, but next time, harder, and lasting—for minutes—for hours!

"If you want me to come by at some point, just phone me."

"Now?" Susan said in a whisper.

Peter looked at his busy children. He thought about their need for his warm presence. He studied his watch.

"Be right there," he said. "Sorry, kids, it's Susan."

Guilt was his companion. But the hug might be there again, and his body ruled his mind, as he left his children, went out and started the car.

CONFESSION

"Dad! Confess!" exclaimed Cassandra the next week.

"What do you mean?" Peter spluttered.

"You know! You're in love!" said Cassandra.

Peter jumped up as if someone had punched a pin in his shoulder. From across the living room, Peter stared out at the ocean, then turned to Cassandra and Henry.

"This is very awkward, but the truth is, I am in love, as you say, but with two women!"

Cassandra, Oliver, and Henry sat back in their chairs with self-satisfied looks.

"Right!" Cassandra whispered in a stage whisper to both of her brothers. "I told you so!"

"So," said Peter, grasping for a way out of this talk.

"So," he repeated to their upturned, expectant faces that reminded him of their little faces years before. He now was an example. How could he have confessed to the sin of loving two people?

"And I'm thinking of moving to Hampstead when you all have left the nest."

"Dad, what? What are you talking about?" whined Cassandra. "Are you saying we won't have any place to come home to on the holidays?"

"You can come to Hampstead!" he reassured her, wondering if there would even be a corner for them.

"Dad, are you going to get married to these women?" Henry asked with a bemused smile.

"No, obviously not. But one of them might come to live with me. I just don't know which one." He laughed nervously.

"Dad! Where will I sleep?" asked Cassandra.

"In Grandpa's flat?" asked Henry, who had walked by it once with Peter.

"That's the idea," said Peter.

"It's too small, isn't it?" said Cassandra, her downcast face giving her insecurity away.

"Cassandra," tried Peter, "Perhaps you'll go abroad and travel the continent during your holidays? You would always be welcomed and at home there. And, if you wanted, I could store your things for you."

"Oh, I see. You are basically kicking me out!" said Cassandra.

"Not at all. You know you three children are my top priority. You always come first!" He looked to see if this old news had sunk in.

"You always say that," said Cassandra. "Anyway, I'm never flying again."

"True," Henry said to Peter, then looked at Cassandra. "Trains?"

Peter said, "You will have a room at the flat. You're young. You can have that reassurance. Promise!"

"Dad, we want to live with you in Hampstead, if you do move to Hampstead!"

Peter was touched by their ignorance of their coming need for independence of him—in particular.

"We will work it out. All I said was, 'I'm in love!'"

"With two women!" said Cassandra in rather a loud voice.

"One of whom will win!" said Henry, rubbing his hands together.

"Not over any of you, my darlings," said Peter. "Now, not to worry. I'll be living here for a couple of years while you find your feet."

"My friends don't want to stay at their parents' houses once they go to uni…," said Henry.

"But they can't afford not to!" said Cassandra.

"Like us," said Henry.

"You can work during the holidays," said Peter.

"WORK?" said Cassandra and Henry in unison.

"Yes, at worst, I could hire you to help me out."

"No, thanks, Dad. I'll wait tables!" said Henry. "We've heard too much of your work phone calls, Dad. We'll find jobs. All our friends will find work somehow. Maybe abroad. I want to travel, anyway."

"Me, too!" said Cassandra.

"Me, too!" said Peter.

"You?" said Cassandra. "Dad! You have to be at home so we can leave you!"

They all laughed. But there was no mother at home that they could leave. Perhaps they all wanted to leave, even Peter; they wanted to leave their dead mother, Peter's dead wife, and all that long history that was hanging around their house that anchored them to the past they needed to forget. It was time for all of them to move on, but they didn't know what that would mean or where they would go. It was time. They sat and looked at each other.

"Tea?" said Peter.

ARRANGEMENTS

Peter had heard stories of women who no longer had their periods, who even had false pregnancies. He glanced at Cassandra's waistline
today as she took off her cardigan. She looked as normal as a teenager
who regularly ate a little more than she should. He remembered being a
nervous teenager himself; he had stopped wanting to eat as a result.

"Hi, Dad," she said with her beautiful smile.

"Tea?" he offered, as usual.

"Not now," she said. "It's too bitter for my stomach."

"Oh?" he said.

She looked at him for longer than usual, like she wanted to say something else.

"Something wrong?" he ventured.

"Not really. Tea just makes me nauseous—even thinking about it."

Peter kept his mouth shut, hoping for more, yet dreading it.

"Do you have much homework?" he said after a short while.

"Not too much. Hamlet, silly man, wasn't he?" she said, flipping through
her satchel and pulling out her notebooks and a copy of Shakespeare's trag-
edies. She was still standing over the table when she stopped and leaned
forward, her hand over her mouth.

Peter got up, pulled out a chair, and guided her to sit down.

"What's going on, love?"

"It's nothing. Just a tummy upset–something I ate at lunch."

Peter so wanted to believe it was nothing. He remembered Jeannie acting exactly this way and feared the possibilities that might last a lifetime. He sat down and felt her forehead.

"No fever," he said. "That's good. What did you have for lunch?" he asked, glancing at the tea kettle as if it might offer her comfort.

"Dad, if you must know, I think I might be pregnant."

Peter steadied himself and lifted his hand away from her forehead. At first, he caught himself with a black thought. 'How could you do this to me, you crazy girl?' Instead, he said, "But you said…."

"I lied," she said, bluntly, looking rather sick.

"Of course. Why wouldn't you? You are sure now, aren't you?"

"Helen knows. She's been helping me work through it."

"Thank goodness for Helen!" he mumbled, grateful that he had supported therapy for Cassandra.

"We're working it out–all possibilities." Cassandra looked at him. He looked at her, trying to keep his look blank, uncommitted, internal, with no obvious bias.

"It's your body, love. It's your life. If he loves you, that's what matters."

"Of course we love each other, Dad. But we're way too young, right?"

Peter felt relieved but tried to hide it.

"We have made arrangements, Dad. Tomorrow."

"Tomorrow?"

"Yes, I am only seven weeks late. It's better to do it right away, right?"

Peter thought in a flash of the long-term consequences of either choice.

"It's your decision, love. I'm supportive of whatever you decide. Can I give you a lift to the doctor's office?"

"That's okay, Dad. Gerald has his dad's car. He's coming to hold my hand."

"Good man," Peter said, relieved. He truly was not in the mood to witness the process.

"Tea here afterwards, then. And bring that young man, too."

"That is very generous of you, Dad. He's a gentleman, a real gentleman."

SCOOTER

Cassandra held the phone and whispered, "I need to postpone this procedure. Yes. One week. Thank you."

The next day, Cassandra turned to Peter, and said, "Daddy, Gerald is coming to pick me up soon."

"On his bicycle?" asked Peter, then added, "Or in his father's car?"

"Not today, Dad. On his new scooter."

"Helmet?" asked Peter.

"I don't know," answered Cassandra.

"Helmet!" insisted Peter.

"I'm going anyway. It's only to town, Dad."

"Helmet or walk!"

"Oh, Dad. You're so...."

"Parental?" he said.

"Fussy!"

"Gerald may be a great driver...."

"Which he is...."

"But there are other mad drivers out there, not paying attention."

The front doorbell rang.

"Don't say 'helmet' or I'll kill you!" Cassandra ran to the front door, paused, smiled, and opened it.

Gerald stood there, two helmets dangling from his right hand.

"Ready?" he asked.

"Yes. Just a mo'," she said, turning her head back to shout down the hallway into the kitchen where Peter hovered with his ear cocked in her direction.

"He has two helmets," she yelled.

"Be careful!" he yelled back in a very parental voice, loud enough for Gerald to get his meaning.

"Yes, sir," Peter heard him say.

Peter watched as Cassandra grabbed Gerald's free arm and looked up at his black, curly hair as they walked outside and over to his scooter.

Peter smiled and waved at his little girl. He glared at Gerald. He felt guilty, but it was as if a ghost of centuries forced him to do it.

"Who are you?" he mumbled to himself. "You're not the bloody king!" Still, she was almost two-months pregnant. It would be his grand-child, for heaven's sake. Yet, he knew, it had to be their decision, not his.

The scooter kicked up a few bits of gravel as it headed out of the driveway and down the steep hill, with steeple-roofed houses lining each side, and clouds shuffling around the blue sky. Peter thought of Jeannie. He remembered their innocent love. He deeply wished that perfect love for Cassandra, so that when the hard times came, which they always would, her memories of her love of Gerald might sustain them.

Peter went back to his chair and looked absently at his watch, not registering the time it said. He was flipping through the pages of *The Sunday Times*, hunting for stories that might throw clues into his current criminal case. It seemed that people were all basically the same. They were lacking in something they felt entitled to, in some desperate way, and were willing to break the law. The women were shoplifters and check forgers; the men were burglars and thieves of larger objects, like televisions and cars. Violence was sometimes a problem, but in most of his cases, the perps had no intention of harming people unless someone got in their way.

Peter remembered a few times when Jeannie seemed crazy, when he had three young children to get off to school and then a job to go to. He remembered waiting too long to pay the electric bill because Jeannie drank their money away that month, and how they had once eaten by candlelight. But mostly he remembered that tempting moment when he began thinking of ways to steal something, so he could get the money to turn the lights back on. He'd seen the results of that in so many people that just could not make it. They drank away the money. Then they felt entitled to get themselves into trouble and landed at the other side of a table, answering his questions in monosyllables.

THE PHONE RANG

At first, Peter was annoyed when Cassandra didn't come home as promised at 11:30 p.m. A vision of Cellini flashed across his mind and disappeared just as quickly. He yawned and looked at his watch. Midnight. He frowned, got up and went to the front door, opened it and stepped out into the foggy night.

All was quiet now. It seemed like the seagulls were asleep, the crickets were asleep, and all the neighboring dogs were asleep. He looked up to see the stars. Fog! He listened for the sound of a scooter pulling two laughing teenagers up the steep incline. But he heard nothing. This quiet moment felt like a warning, like it was announcing something and preparing one for the worst. He shivered and walked back inside, closing the door. A watercolor painting from the hallway wall crashed to the floor from its twenty-year-old deteriorating hook, and the glass shattered on the floor.

"Damn!" muttered Peter, going to the kitchen and picking up the broom and dustpan.

He couldn't help it. He cocked his ear for that scooter sound as he swept up the glass.

The phone rang in the kitchen.

Peter dropped the dustpan, and the broken glass fell out again on the hallway floor. He ran and picked up the phone.

"Cassandra?" he said.

"Is this her father?"

"It is!" Peter tried to be calm.

"I'm afraid…," said the voice.

Peter started yelling, "NO!"

"I'm afraid she's been in an accident."

"And?" Peter choked in a ridiculously calm voice.

There was a long pause. Is she dead? Tell me!

"She's alive, but in a coma," the messenger blurted out.

"Where?" Peter asked, choking on his own saliva.

"Here in Brighton at the hospital."

"Can I come right now?"

"Please come right away!"

Peter slammed down the phone, dashed down the hallway, grabbed his coat, kicking the dustpan at the wall. Then he kicked the wall.

"I bloody told her!" he yelled at the front door as he flung it open, slammed it behind him, and dashed to his car. Then he remembered that they had helmets.

In Cassandra's hospital room, Peter sat, face drawn, and held up his chin with his tired hands, looking at his very quiet daughter. No broken legs or arms. No chest wounds–just a coma–just a bloody coma! He wiped his eyes and berated himself for ever letting her go on that horrible scooter.

Gerald had lived and had a broken arm and a broken hip. Peter could not bear to visit him, even though Gerald was right there in the same hospital.

"Oh, my God!" Peter said aloud. "What if she never comes round, and eventually gives birth? Then this bloody miserable scooter boyfriend becomes my grandchild's father!" Then he remembered she was only two months pregnant–time enough to see what might happen.

Peter looked at his peaceful Cassandra. He willed her to wake up. He even prayed that she would just open her eyes and say, "Hi, Daddy!" This was too much like Jeannie all over again.

Peter really did not think he could be pleasant and sympathetic to Gerald, but just in case, he realized he had better go see him first thing. Cassandra was clearly not going to wake up tonight.

He checked his watch. It was now 2 a.m. He stood up straight, his jaw firm and stoic, and resolved to do whatever was needed for his Cassandra.

Gerald was fast asleep when Peter looked in. Peter left him to sleep, drove home, and planned to bring the boys back with him in the morning.

COMA

The next morning Peter brought Henry and Oliver but decided to go into Gerald's room alone at first. He asked the boys to hang back until he could gauge the situation. Gerald was awake.

"Oh, hello…um, Mr. Evans. So bloody sorry," said Gerald.

"Hello, Gerald. Sorry, sorry," Peter said, seeing again how badly Gerald had been injured. "Looks like you took quite a spill."

"How's Cassandra?" asked Gerald.

Peter liked that. Gerald actually was thinking about someone else besides himself.

"Sorry to say, she's in a coma," said Peter.

"Oh," Gerald said, looking down. "Bloody hell!"

"But you are quite a mess here!" joked Peter.

"Can't even scratch my ear!" said Gerald. "But did they say how long she might be in a coma?"

"They don't actually know. But let's say a day or two," said Peter.

"You're totally making that up, aren't you, just to make me have hope?"

"No, I'm making that up so I have hope."

"Oh, sorry. Of course. Could you please hold that glass for me so I can sip some water?"

"Of course," said Peter, lifting the glass and pointing the straw towards Gerald's lips. "Here you go."

Peter felt a moment of confusion between being angry and being glad Gerald had survived. He held the glass and Gerald sipped the water through the straw.

"Thank you," Gerald said. "Mr. Evans, I want to say how sorry I am about all this. At least we were wearing our helmets. It was totally the other driver's fault. It was, honestly."

"It's all right. When I saw you had brought two helmets, I guessed you'd be a responsible driver. Can't predict the other drivers we'll meet out there, can we?"

"I'm frightened that I'll never want to ride that scooter again," Gerald said, looking small and dejected. "That is, if it is not totally messed up."

Peter couldn't keep his fatherly side from coming out. "Of course, you are. But that will pass. As soon as you heal, whenever that is, you'll get right back on that scooter, and you'll start riding it again. But not with Cassandra!"

Gerald looked even more dejected.

"Until everybody is back to normal," added Peter. "Her brothers are waiting outside. Want to see them?"

"Will they punch me?" asked Gerald.

Peter smiled, got up, and opened the door. The boys hovered just outside.

"Hey!" said Gerald, moving his plastered arm a little.

"Look at you!" said Henry, walking in.

"Bit of a mess!" said Oliver, walking right up to the foot of the bed.

"I'll live!" said Gerald.

"Cassandra's in a coma," said Oliver.

"But she'll get better soon," said Peter.

"She will?" asked Oliver.

All three boys studied Peter's face. Peter had no idea. But he well knew how important hope could be.

"Of course. A couple of days, most likely," he lied. He made it up as he went along, like a good father.

"Cheerio, then!" they all said after a few more jokes, and then all three filed out the door.

A thought flew through Peter's mind. "Why couldn't she have broken limbs, and he be in a coma?"

"Oh, hell! I'm getting really petty," he said aloud.

"What?" Oliver asked.

"I said, let's go out to lunch! Fish and chips?"

"Yes, please!" they said.

"And an ice cream afterwards," Peter added.

"Maybe she'll come round tomorrow?" asked Oliver.

"Hope so," said Peter, arm around his younger son. "Fish and chips it is!"

"And ice cream!" said Oliver.

BLINK TWICE

"Even if my dreams came true…," mumbled Cassandra.

Angela stood up, her mouth dropping open, while Michael grabbed her hand.

"She's talking!" said Oliver, placing his arm on Michael's. Peter looked away from the nurse and into Cassandra's face, so calm and serene.

"Dreams," he said. "Your dreams!"

There was a moment where they all hovered over her and waited, and hoped, and held their communal breaths—even the nurse.

But Cassandra again lay silent and still. Nothing more was to be given as a jewel of hope. They started breathing again, eyes down, with perhaps a tear surreptitiously being wiped away from the nurse's calm face.

"Well, there's hope!" said Michael, his arm around Angela.

"Of course, there's hope!" said Peter. "Always was—these things take their own time."

"What do you know?" blurted out Henry. "Oh, sorry, Dad. Right…Mum."

Peter chose to ignore the remark, though memories of Jeannie's last days haunted this room now. He thought he would keel over and die if Cassandra didn't pull through.

Peter turned back to the nurse, and they walked over to the door.

"She's pregnant," Peter whispered.

"It could be a false positive," the nurse offered.

"No. She's pregnant."

"Pregnant!" yelled Oliver.

"Then we have even more reason to hope for a good outcome," said the nurse.

"Dad!" both sons said.

"Sorry. Silly idiot." Peter went over and stroked Cassandra's cheek.

"We'll welcome whatever comes," he said. The word abortion bounced in his mind, but he couldn't bring it up. Not now.

"They could abort it," said Oliver. Henry gave him a dirty look.

"Well, they could!" protested Oliver.

They all looked at each other. Who would take care of a baby if Cassandra fell back into a coma forever? Peter thought of Gerald, who would be its father. Could he do it? Certainly, Peter had managed all these years. But Gerald was nineteen and looking forward to university.

"Oh, God!" Peter said.

"Dad. We can wait," said Oliver. "It's her decision. She's obviously coming round, isn't she?" Oliver looked at the nurse for encouragement and hope.

"We can't say right now," she said. "People in comas can blurt out words, but they might still remain in a coma."

All faces turned back to Cassandra.

"Cassandra?" said Oliver. "Can you hear me? Blink twice if you can."

They all studied her eyes in silence.

She did not even blink once.

She lay there in her own land. Who knew what her dreams were, or even if she dreamed? Did people in comas dream? Peter studied her eye movements–back and forth under the lids. That meant dreams. That meant brain activity. Surely, she would come round. Peter reached for her limp hand and held it firmly. He squeezed it twice. He meant, "Love you."

She squeezed it back twice.

"She squeezed my hand!" shouted Peter. "I squeezed hers and she squeezed mine back—twice!"

The nurse shoed them all away and started studying Cassandra's face and glanced up at her medical numbers. She took Cassandra's same hand and squeezed it. No reaction. Peter willed for the repetition of her squeeze, but apparently it was only meant for him. He moved back into place and took Cassandra's hand from the nurse in silent understanding and squeezed it twice.

All faces leaned forward.

The sun flirted with the clouds outside the window.

Cassandra squeezed his hand twice.

JUST FINE

Peter opened Cassandra's palm towards his face, leaned down, and kissed it three times.

"Dad?" Cassandra said, blinking rapidly.

"Cassandra!" shouted Oliver.

"Shhh!" said the nurse.

"Sorry," said Oliver.

"Okay, everybody," Peter said, "Relax. She's going to be fine, aren't you?"

"Hi, Dad! Where am I?" she said.

"In hospital," he said.

"Am I dying?"

"No, silly. Just banged up a bit," said Oliver.

"Am I?" she said, looking at her hand. "I was in an accident, wasn't I?"

"You and Gerald," said Peter.

"Is he okay?" she asked, a line creasing her forehead.

"Sort of," said Henry.

"Broke all kinds of bones," said Oliver.

"Oh, no!" Cassandra said. "But he's alive!"

"Alive and hurting pretty badly, I'm afraid," said Peter.

"Oh, I must see him. Where is he?"

"Not yet, my love. He's in this hospital, but you've been in a coma."

"Have I? Can I look in a mirror?"

The nurse pulled a hand mirror out of the drawer. She said it seemed to be one of the first requests people made once they realized what had happened to them.

Cassandra held it up to see purple bruises with some yellow blending in. "Oh, God! I'm a bloody mess! How can you bear to look at me?"

"We are so happy to look at your lovely face now!" said Peter. "We don't care about your hair or your bruises. We care that you are alive!"

"And still have a brain," blurted Oliver.

"Shush!" said Henry.

"The doctor's coming," said the nurse. "May I ask you all to wait outside for a few minutes?"

"Can I stay here? I'm her father and only parent," Peter said.

"We will call you right back in, but I'm sure this young lady might want a bit of privacy with the doctor. Right, me love?"

"It's okay. Just for a minute, Dad. Then you can come back in. Don't go far! And don't forget, I'm alive!"

"There's a lovely waiting room for you all just across the hallway," said the nurse. "I'll call you back very soon, not to worry."

They all followed each other dutifully across the hallway and sat down to wait.

"Everything's all right if you live through scooter accidents with no helmets on!" said Oliver.

"Remember, they had helmets on," said Peter, adding, "They're both alive, thank God." He wiped away a tear that would not stay back and stole a look at his two boys—his young men on the brink of manhood.

TAKING THE PAINTINGS DOWN

After a few more days, Cassandra, still pregnant, went home from the hospital. Soon enough, Gerald was back at his home, on crutches. Cassandra said he was still fighting all the time with his mother. Peter sat musing about their accident. Was it possible that Cellini's bad luck curse might still be plaguing his family?

Angela was a soft-spoken woman, especially these days. Peter liked this version of his mother as opposed to the one who yelled for him to get going to school.

And, of course, as crazy as his uncle–rather, his father, Michael–was, Peter felt a warmth in their joint presence, pleased they had at last found and acknowledged their union that went back nine months before Peter's birth.

Peter decided he would stay in Rottingdean for now. The magnificent view of the ocean was worth the extra expense of bits of the roof being blown off in storms, or branches crashing into his large windows.

Soon, of course, he repeated to himself, all his children would be off to university.

Peter looked around the walls at his paintings. They were old, as paintings all tend to become, living in their own special rectangle on the walls all through his house. Each time he'd been persuaded to purchase one, it was way beyond their budget. Jeannie and he had argued: new shoes for the kids in September or this new painting? It was a ridiculous choice, but Peter was amused at how many times irrationality and beauty had won over practicality. Each painting was a moment in time through his life, and his life with Jeannie: Paris, flowers, ocean views, a dancer in watercolor, Hampstead High Street, Hampstead Heath, and a self-portrait from the old artist, still there at Brighton Pier.

All at once, Peter, echoing a lonely moment down the hall, reached out his long arms and began removing one painting after the other, every single one down the hallway walls. He walked back through the hallway and stacked them, right side up, by the back door, then stomped down the empty hallway into the living room and started lifting each of the larger paintings off their hooks. One by one, each one carefully cradled in the curled fingers of each hand, he strode back down the hallway, with one painting tucked under his left arm, and the other under his right arm. Then he stacked them one against the other. Before long, every room downstairs had bare walls, complete with slightly lighter hued rectangles where the paintings had lived for years.

Peter did question his sanity. What was he thinking? Why did he do that? What would the children say? Would they be upset? Would Jeannie haunt him?

No—he did it, and he was happy. He had no idea at all what made him do it. So, he went into the kitchen, and with a cursory glance over at the line of stacked up paintings, he put the kettle on.

"I'm home, Dad!" shouted Cassandra, slamming the front door.

"Hello, love. Cuppa tea?" he shouted back.

"Dad! What have you done to Mom's paintings?" she said, coming into the kitchen.

"They're here, love," he said, showing them stacked up by the back door. "We need to paint the walls." He'd made it up on the spot, but he was rather pleased that he did it so easily. He smiled.

"Dad? Are you sure?"

"Of course, my love. Look at them. Can you help me, or is it too soon?"

"I'm not all better, Dad. Maybe you could hire someone?" she said, making her way up the stairs.

"Right. Sorry, my love."

"Supper's ready!" Peter shouted twenty minutes later, putting the teapot and cups on the table, and wondering about colors. He'd do it himself, then.

LIKE A FAMILY

Peter looked closely at Cassandra. It was like something was blocking his hearing. Surely, she was joking. Surely, she wasn't pregnant, and surely, they were not raising it in this house he was planning to leave. Surely not.

"You are having me on, aren't you?" he said.

"What do you mean, Dad?" she replied.

"Are you seriously pregnant?"

"Well, I was, so stop fretting like an old lady."

Peter jumped up and gave Cassandra a kiss on the cheek.

"Dad. I hoped you would have been just as excited if I'd kept it!"

"Of course! Of course!" he said almost gleefully.

"Dad?"

"Yes, my love?"

"You're a bloody liar!"

"True, true. It's just that, well, did you notice the paintings are still down?"

"And you're waiting for the painter, right?"

"Yes. I told you. But part of the reason is that I'm going to live in London at some point."

There, he had said it again. It just came out, and he'd somehow made the decision, right as he said it.

"What? Leave our house? Can I live here still, Gerald and me?" she whined.

"Well, not really. Gerald? Can't afford two places, especially with London prices."

"Dad, you said you can live in Michael's and your old flat in Hampstead. No rent!"

"But my income will suffer, trying to pay for two places. I'd have to pay Michael, as well, because he can't be without the rent his tenants were paying."

"You always said Grandpa charged too little, so he won't miss it that much." She plunked herself down into a chair and pushed her mug towards the teapot.

"Who's going to make my tea?" she pouted.

"I'm not leaving until you go to uni, not to worry," Peter said, pouring her tea.

"I should have kept the baby," she mumbled. "Then you wouldn't move."

"Times change. Don't go getting pregnant again now!"

Cassandra put two teaspoons full of sugar into her tea and stirred.

"Dad, I don't want to leave this house: I'm too young! Gerald can move in, right?" she begged.

"No, he can't," said Peter.

"He hates his mum. And she hates him! She drinks like a fish."

"Well, as they say in the good old USA, 'That's not my problem.'"

"Oh, Dad," said Cassandra. "That's so American. Let's be a family."

"A what?" he blurted.

"Like a family."

"We haven't been a true family for years, my love," said Peter, crunching on a biscuit.

"What do you mean?"

"Well, you know, Jeannie dying and all that," he said.

"Dad. You are grossly old-fashioned. A family is whatever you decide it is, right? So, if Gerald moves in, he is part of our family," she stated firmly.

"He's not moving in, and that's that!"

"His mum just chucked him out. He's just got me and his bashed-up scooter now."

"Not my problem!" insisted Peter, now rather concerned, but unwilling to jeopardize his glimpse of freedom.

"Where's he supposed to live, then, on the streets?"

"Legally, with his family until he's, I dunno, eighteen, is it?"

"He's nineteen, Dad. He got a new job!"

"Then he can rent a room, just like normal people do," said Peter, almost hyperventilating and feeling cornered like a little mouse before a crouching cat.

"Anyway, Dad, he's on his way over with his toothbrush, so please, please, be nice, just for a few days," she said, putting her hand on his shoulder and giving him a little girl look.

TOO YOUNG

Gerald arrived with a large backpack and a smile after leaning forwards in order to conquer the steep hill on his bashed-up scooter. When Cassandra answered the door, Gerald dropped his pack and opened his arms. Peter looked away. Surely this was not happening to him. Surely Gerald, who was a nice enough young man, really, would be a short-term guest and not a tenant—or worse, a relative!

Gerald had the presence of mind to step forward with his hand outstretched and his face producing a genuine smile. "Thank you so much, Mr. Evans. I wasn't sure if you'd be favorable to a house guest, but Cassandra assured me you would be very welcoming. Very generous of you."

"Well," spluttered Peter. "It's fine. Just make yourself at home. Tea?"

Peter hated feeling caught in this web of fatherly love. He rustled around with the kettle and the teapot, trying to decide whether Gerald's arrival deserved real tea leaves or tea bags. Gerald should be grateful for the teapot, anyway, and not just a mug with a teabag thrown into the microwave!

The three of them sat down to discuss the weather and avoid the obvious.

"So," said Peter, "I hear you have a new job." Peter hated sounding like a prospective father-in-law, but the words came tumbling out like they had from the first caveman.

"Yes," replied Gerald. "Just for a few months' trial, but then, if they approve of me, it will be permanent."

Peter thought of his boys, both working part time, pushing through their studies somehow, and probably getting stoned at the same time. He wondered now if Gerald did drugs?

"So," Peter said, "Are you reading anything interesting?"

"Dad!" exclaimed Cassandra. "Who has time to read, work, and study?"

"Indeed!" said Peter. "Well, in that case, what are you studying?"

"Actually, I'm taking a term off. We thought…."

Cassandra gave him a hard look.

"I mean, I thought we might need a little time in case Cassandra was having a baby–which she wasn't," he added.

"Which she isn't, right?" Peter said rather earnestly.

"Which she isn't," Gerald affirmed.

"Is not!" Peter said.

"Not!" said Cassandra.

"Yet," said Gerald.

"What?" said Peter.

"Gerald–I told you!" Cassandra said, frowning.

"Haven't you two decided to get rid…, I mean, not to have it?" Peter said, covering his mouth for being as blunt as Oliver.

"We're trying to decide," said Cassandra.

"We're too young, we know," said Gerald.

"Yes, you are! It seems to me that if you can't figure out contraception, you can't really be ready for the responsibility of parenthood! Now, why not make those arrangements, as you had planned?"

"We did," said Cassandra.

"You did?" said Peter.

"But we postponed them for a week," said Cassandra.

"A week?" said Peter, wondering what a whole week could do to their decisions.

"Dad," she said, "It won't make any difference, will it?"

YOU KNEW

Peter felt that the end of his life by the sea was beckoning uncomfortably, like a white witch with red fingernails. Looking back at the moment when he started taking down his paintings, he remembered feeling like some magic hands had lifted up decades of treasured art. He realized now that when he walked by them, he hardly ever saw them.

Peter went into the kitchen and stood for a while, looking at the paintings all stacked up on the backroom floor like they were for sale in the gallery on Hampstead High Street. He imagined strangers pawing through his treasures and offering a staggeringly lower price than the ones on offer.

He walked back into the sitting room. It felt lifeless, dark, and unloved, like the day Jeannie had died. Peter couldn't help fuming at the house painter that he had finally hired, who kept postponing his work dates.

Peter sat in the kitchen most of the time, next to the kettle, the teapot, and the old ticking clock.

Where were they now? They should be home for tea by now. Peter loved punctuality regarding teatime. It was in his bones, as were Big Ben's chimes on the BBC. It was time for tea, and that was just how it was. Peter felt he must be of the older generation by now, even though his parents were quite alive, possibly planning some dreadful, exciting new adventure. He checked his old watch, its arms delightfully moving around the numbers, as watches were meant to do. It was too quiet. One of them should have returned by now. He put the kettle on, hoping that the whistle of the boiling water might hurry them home, like a Pavlovian dog and its bell. Peter almost started drooling.

The door. The slam. The sigh. The coat on the rack; a dropping of a satchel. Life was again entering Peter's rather quiet existence.

"Hey, Dad?" said Cassandra.

"Tea?" he answered.

"Not now. I'm going out with Gerald as soon as he gets home."

"Oh, very nice, too! You two have weathered this thing awfully well."

"Well, Dad, if we're going to be parents, this has been a big test. Seems we've passed it!"

"Parents?" he mumbled.

"You knew, didn't you?"

"Well, I knew, but I thought…."

"Don't be silly. We're old enough, Dad."

"What about…."

"University? I'll still go. They have a nursery there."

Peter looked up at his youngest child, who clearly had no idea whatsoever about raising children and trying to read a book longer than two minutes at a time.

"I hope Gerald doesn't think you're going to do all the housework?"

"Dad! Don't be old-fashioned! It's different these days. Fathers pitch in, like you and Mum."

"I was pretty good before Mum died, but afterwards is when I realized how much she had carried without me ever noticing it."

"Like I say, Dad, times have changed."

"Nappies still need changing, speaking of change, same as in the olden days."

"Yes, but, no safety pins and you don't have to wash them anymore."

"True, true." He poured his own cup of tea, marveling at the lack of imagination and experience of youth. He really couldn't complain. It was just as it was.

"Where are you going to raise your baby?"

"Here, of course!" she said. "Right, Dad?"

What could he say?

He sighed as his dream of moving into Hampstead vanished.

LAWANDA

A light rain had become hail in two minutes. Peter slung his scarf across his face and breathed warm air into his nose. It had been months since the airplane accident and then the scooter accident. Things were back to normal–except Cassandra was now eight months pregnant. And his dreams of living in Hampstead had almost totally faded into the mist.

Peter was working hard, trying to solve strange cases that he could never have imagined in his youth. It seemed that a steady stream of illegal immigrants were hiding in sailboats arriving over the Channel from France. There was now a regular police van parked by the Rottingdean jetty to arrest them and take them to London. Peter had to be available in Rottingdean to question them. For most of them, their English was non-existent, but he, at least, managed their names and ages, using fingers for counting and a strip of the alphabet he had written down on his pad for them to point at. There were people arriving from all over: the Middle East, Africa, Lebanon. The list went on. Peter started to learn keywords in their languages.

But at this point, back at home, he was also dragging out baby things from their storage space in preparation for the coming baby. Nobody had ever dumped the stuff. There never seemed to be time. The pram just needed a little oiling and cleaning, and the clothes of all sizes needed to be sorted through. The safety pins, of course, were indeed useless.

A boat arrived that day, and just slowly getting off it was a heavily pregnant young woman, who called herself Lawanda—from somewhere in Africa. Peter applied for permission to take her personally to the hospital to get her a checkup. He felt a severe strain of concern at her precarious living situation, and obvious lack of things that go with having a baby.

"May I ask where you plan to go now?" Peter asked her.

Lawanda spoke beautiful English with a slight accent.

"I have no relatives at all left back home in Africa. My family have all died in wars and from diseases. I am now alone."

Peter swallowed as he glanced at her very pregnant stomach—not unlike Cassandra's.

"I do have a distant relative in London. I have an old address for them, but no phone number."

"How old are you, Lawanda?" he asked, his pen poised.

"Seventeen, sir," she said.

Peter was shocked—same age as Cassandra. He melted immediately. This young girl was as pregnant as Cassandra! She needed a home immediately. It happened so quickly that he hardly knew who he was. He saw her holding her stomach with one hand and her rucksack with the other and he knew he really must make all the endless, but proper—if temporary—legal arrangements.

"I have a daughter your age living with me who will soon have a baby. Why not come and live with us at our house for a while?"

Lawanda smiled, and Peter could see tears in her eyes. "I would love to stay with you until I find my relatives in London. Thank you so very much!"

Peter drove Lawanda straight up to his house. As soon as Cassandra and Lawanda met, they bonded right away.

"My, my! It looks like we are going to have our babies on the same day!" said Cassandra. Was there a grasp of this advanced state of pregnancy, that, clearly, only another woman just as pregnant could understand?

"It's kicking!" said Lawanda, grabbing Cassandra's hand and placing it on her protruding stomach.

"Mine, too!" said Cassandra, grabbing Lawanda's hand and placing it on her own belly.

Their faces, with their wide, happy eyes and broad smiles, said it all: life!

THE NEW FAMILY

Peter guided his children and Lawanda over to the table with the white tablecloth where dinner at this restaurant was set for ten. He brushed a stray hair from his new brown corduroy jacket, which, in fact, he'd bought at the local outdoor market. It was a bargain, obviously never worn, and it certainly looked new.

"I have to warn you about my dad," Gerald whispered to Peter. "He has a rather rude mouth on him."

"I'll make a note of that!" Peter whispered back.

Cassandra got to sit at the head of the table, and Gerald sat next to her. Lawanda sat right next to Cassandra on the other side. They exchanged looks, like their babies were kicking, reminding them of their babies' pending arrival.

Henry and Oliver hardly looked at Cassandra's stomach. It was all very clear who had done the deed, but their British training probably couldn't stop them from being entertained by silent thoughts about which position it was conceived in–and Lawanda! Well, that was done in some faraway land, and was too hard to imagine.

Peter tried desperately not to dwell on that sort of meandering thought, but it entertained him unwillingly, nevertheless!

Gerald's mother, Mary, entered like she was some famous American actress from the 1940s. She was all lipstick and sparkly earrings and had clearly walked directly over from the hairdresser's down the lane. Peter felt the necessity of catering to her need for recognition, and his thoughts swelled around the reason she had kicked Gerald out six months previously.

"He's coming shortly," she gestured behind her.

Gerald's father, John, struggled in the door with his cane. He was far too young for a cane, but there was some rumor about an accident five years earlier. Nobody seemed to notice his cane. Gerald carried a cane still but had a way of hiding it so that it wasn't noticeable. He'd need it another week; hardly ever used it now.

Gerald's two younger sisters, Dolly and Tessa, floated in on their egos, fluttering and primping and making sure everybody was watching. They duly patted Cassandra and Lawanda's protruding stomachs, made high-pitched cooing sounds, and found their seats.

Peter was slightly shocked at having this new family thrust upon him. Hampstead, glittering in the far distance, would still have to wait. He saw himself as a grandfather-to-be and a handy babysitter for these very young parents-to-be.

The waiter was pouring water, then wine. Gerald's parents had finished their first glass of wine before Peter had time to offer his speech and raise his glass. Nobody mentioned it, but Peter thought he heard Gerald mumble under his breath, "Here we go!"

Peter stood up and cleared his throat. The waiter arrived with warm bread.

"Well, here we all are," said Peter. "…a new family, offering our congratulations to the new couple and their pending arrival! And congratulations to Lawanda, as well!"

Cassandra smoothed her protruding belly and looked down, then smiled at Lawanda, whose arm lightly touched her own belly.

"Got knocked up, then, didn't she?" said John, nodding at Peter.

"Dad!" scolded Gerald.

"Well, it's true, isn't it?"

Peter raised his glass urgently. "Cheers!" he said.

Mary said, "Well, it's not like she didn't have a bit of help, then, is it?"

Peter said, "We wish Gerald and Cassandra and Lawanda all the very best!" He raised his glass higher.

"I'll drink to that, and the best of British luck to you! You'll be needing it!" said John.

"To the Queen!" said Oliver.

"To Cassandra and Gerald! And Lawanda!" said Peter, raising his glass yet again.

"I'll drink to that!" said Mary.

"And I will, and all!" said John, raising his glass.

Cassandra burst out laughing for no reason at all. Gerald looked upset but caught her humor and started laughing with her. Lawanda was hiding her mouth, trying to stifle her own mirth. All at once, the laughter caught on, and everybody began laughing.

Peter noticed Gerald's parents had already finished off their third glasses of wine.

ENOUGH

How could they keep knocking them back like that? Peter only sipped for each new, "*Cheers!*" He searched all their faces and particularly the ones who had chucked Gerald out of (but rather, that Gerald had escaped from), a situation of drunken parents. One day Peter would find out the truth. But, for now, it was all jolly and pretend.

"It's getting late," Peter said.

"No, it's not!" said Mary. "Time for another!"

"Sorry, I have to be up early for work," Peter said, inwardly cringing at the size of the upcoming bill. He signaled the waiter for the bill with the usual scribble hand sign. When the waiter approached with the bill, John held up his glass in the waiter's face.

The waiter looked at Peter. Peter gently shook his head while John shoved his glass at the waiter's nose and actually hit it.

"Bloody hell!" said the waiter, backing away.

"Sorry! Sorry!" said Peter.

The waiter stood a safe distance away. Peter got up and walked over to comfort him, all the while slipping enough pounds into the waiter's hands to mollify him.

"Nutcase!" said John.

"Dad! Calm down! You've had enough!" said Gerald.

"Nobody tells me I've had enough!" said John, standing up, scraping his chair away and advancing towards the waiter.

Peter stepped between them and used his best detective resources, not to mention fatherly instincts, and said, in a voice loud enough to wake the seagulls on the roof, "Did you check the pools, then, John?"

"The pools?" said John, well distracted, his eyes wide.

"Maybe you've won! Shall we have a look-see? Maybe we've struck it rich!" All the while, Peter had his hand on John's back and was guiding him away from the waiter and towards the exit.

"You bet on them, right?"

"'Course I did!" he spluttered, digging into his pocket. "Got me ticket right here in me coat, somewhere."

Just before they both exited the door, Peter slipped his credit card to Henry, who finished the transaction with the waiter.

Cassandra and Lawanda staggered out of their chairs and out the door of the restaurant.

In a few minutes, they were all outside, taking in the brisk ocean air. Peter and John were singing a sailor's song, no pools receipt yet discovered. Mary waltzed over and joined in. By all the giggling of Gerald, Cassandra, and Lawanda, walking behind them, no one would have suspected that Peter was feeling sick to his stomach, and thinking, "Oh, God, what has Cassandra gotten us all into?" He hoped for a split second that she would miscarry right in the middle of the chorus.

Peter looked around to see who might be looking at them all, and who might be wondering if they were thinking the same dreadful thoughts, when out popped Mrs. MacBride from the pub doors.

"Hello, me loves!" she said with a smile. And to Peter's astonishment, she joined in singing. It seemed she was a meadowlark, and light on her Irish feet. Well, at least she wouldn't be offended. Peter sighed and sang, only wishing the evening would end.

"You all right, love?" he whispered in Cassandra's ear.

"I don't know," she said, rubbing her vast belly.

"What?" Peter asked.

"It hurts," she said.

"Me, too!" said Lawanda.

GOING TO HOSPITAL

As they all made their way to the cars, Peter suddenly thought of the Cellini silver cups and their accompanying bad luck. And then he thought of Michael and Angela, always arm-in-arm, who were talking with sparkles in their eyes. To look at them, no one would guess they were thieves as Michael stepped off the curb, attending to Cassandra's need for his arm. They always looked like a conservative couple with a traditional past—no threats of prison, no accidental fatherhood and years of hideous silence, with Michael visiting Catherine in prison—just two harmless people enjoying themselves with no cares in the world. Peter remembered so many scenes through his detective life where people who ended up in jail had looked thoroughly innocent and quite normal.

Peter shook himself out of his reverie and tended to Cassandra. He wondered if Michael and Angela had new plans for a trip to Italy. Wasn't that a word he caught? Tickets, *tickets*. Cassandra tripped and would have fallen, but Peter and Michael held her fast, grabbing Lawanda's arms while trying to sound hearty.

"There we go," Peter repeated.

"Shut up, Dad, I'm not a child!" said Cassandra.

"Sorry, love, just concerned," he murmured.

149

"It seems better," she assured them all as they strained their communal ears to hear what was going on.

"Oh, no!" screamed Cassandra a moment later, grabbing her stomach.

Peter recognized the beginning of her labor and decided to take immediate action. He opened the car door and said, "Get in! Get in! Gently does it!" Gerald helped her inside, then ran around the car and climbed in. Peter ran around and got into the driver's seat.

"See you later," yelled Peter. "We're off to the hospital!"

"Should I come?" asked Lawanda.

The look on Peter's face told her to go home.

The doors slammed as they sped off towards Brighton. Within minutes, the traffic was at a standstill. There was an accident ahead, apparently.

Cassandra moaned, making a very low sound that was primeval.

"I'm having it!" she yelled. Peter pulled over to the side, jumped out, and flung the back door open.

Cassandra lay on Gerald's lap. His face was ashen, and perhaps he was crying. It was hard to see, exactly.

"No worries, Cassandra," Peter comforted. "We'll put on the cop flashers and skip this mess!"

He got back into the car and put on his hazards and flashing lights and sped along on the wrong side of the road towards the hospital.

She groaned again, long and loud. Peter prayed: *Oh Lord, make it wait!* He had Gerald phone the hospital to let them know they were arriving.

They pulled up to the hospital where a wheelchair was waiting. Several people in hospital garb helped Cassandra into the wheelchair. As she sat there, all Peter could hear was that haunting moan.

"Hurry!" he said to the hospital employees.

Heavy panting poured from Cassandra's mouth. "It's coming! I can feel it!"

"No, no, no!" said Peter.

"What, Dad?" she said.

"Nothing! You're going to give birth whenever nature has planned it. Just let it be. You are in good hands now!" Peter had once delivered a baby on duty in similar circumstances, but it was not his own child's.

The wheelchair was pushed into the birthing room. They let Gerald in, but Peter sat in the waiting room remembering Jeannie with that same moan and that same fear, and the same result: a baby!

Hours later, as Peter sat slumped, half-asleep in the waiting room, a nurse came in and Peter was told to take them home. It was, apparently, a false alarm.

"Let's hope Lawanda is in one piece, as it were!" said Gerald, helping Cassandra into the back seat, then climbing in on the other side, stealing a glance at her enormous stomach, then putting his arm around her shoulders.

A MOAN!

A day later, Cassandra started yelling, and her voice was louder than Peter had ever heard it. Then Lawanda chimed in. Peter threw down his newspaper and rushed into the kitchen. Both Cassandra and Lawanda were holding their stomachs.

"Oh, no!" shouted Peter.

"Yes!" yelled Cassandra.

"Oh, yes!" yelled Lawanda.

They both staggered into the living room, gripping their stomachs. Peter dialed the hospital for an ambulance. Both of them were seriously in labor, he told them. Best not to try to get to them to the hospital in the car, he was told.

"Why didn't you tell me earlier?" he scolded Cassandra, glaring at Lawanda.

In between pants, Cassandra said she didn't realize what was happening and figured it was another false alarm. "I didn't want to bother you again!"

"Where's Gerald?" Peter asked, frowning.

"I don't know!" Cassandra said, then yelled.

"Aren't you supposed to pant and count instead of yelling?" Peter said. Both girls yelled at him at the same time.

"All right, all right! They're on their way. Calm down!" Peter immediately realized he shouldn't have said that when he saw Cassandra's face
form a scowl that she couldn't complete as she gripped her stomach.

"It's coming!" she yelled.

"Me, too!" said Lawanda.

"Wait!" yelled Peter.

Cassandra was lying back on the couch, and Lawanda was stretched
out in the easy chair. Peter heard the loud panting.

"Oh, God!" he mumbled.

"What?" said Cassandra.

"I said, the ambulance is coming," he said.

"They'd better hurry," said Cassandra.

Peter strained to hear the siren, the one he hated that sounded like
the ones in American films. But he heard only panting. And now a moan.
A moan! That's when it's coming out! He distinctly remembered that
sound from Jeannie. It was a deep growl, so animal-sounding, and completely uncontrollable. All he could do was imagine holding those babies
back. Of course, he'd learned to deliver a baby in a detective class, but
that was a doll, not his daughter's baby! And, he remembered once again,
that one time he had delivered someone else's baby.

"Hot water!" yelled Cassandra.

Peter was grateful for instructions and ran to the kitchen, filled up the
tea kettle and two large pans with water and put them on the stove.

He ran back into the living room.

"Sheets, flannels, towels!" Cassandra panted.

Peter ran to the linen closet and grabbed a pile of whatever he
touched and ran it into the living room.

Just then, Gerald pushed the front door open. "Oh, my God!"

"Looks like they're having them now!" said Peter.

"Where's the bloody ambulance? Hello, my love," he said to Cassandra,
pecking her forehead.

"Hello, you!" he added to Lawanda, who was panting in rhythm with
Cassandra.

Peter did not want to be doing this. He swore at the National Health
Service, he swore at the doctors, the drivers, and the inevitable traffic.

"All right, you two," he said, acting like he was in control.

They looked at him, awaiting instructions.

"I'll catch Cassandra's," said Gerald.

"Of course," said Peter. He looked at Lawanda. "I'll catch Lawanda's."

"It's coming!" yelled Cassandra.

"Mine's coming, too!" yelled Lawanda.

Peter ran into the kitchen and back and forth with the hot water. He wasn't quite sure what it was for, but he figured it would become clear.

And then that moaning came: low, animal, long, slow. Lawanda had slid onto the floor, turned over and was now on her hands and knees, pushing her baby out with a moan. Peter decided he had to look, and she would forgive him later. Her baby was crowning.

"It's coming!" she said, then moaned another long, low moan.

Gerald was gaping at Cassandra's spread legs, acting ready for the baby like he was catching a ball. A long, low moan came from her mouth as she pushed hard. The two babies were born almost at the same time. Peter finally used that hot water as he scalded the scissors to cut the umbilical cords.

The two men looked at each other as they washed the babies' bodies and faces, then swaddled them and put them both down next to each other in the armchair.

Then the young women were panting, preparing to push out the placenta. Peter remembered that part. He couldn't understand what all the noise was about. Weren't the babies born? He looked at the scene. Blood and sheets and towels and pans. Two women pushing again, and two babies now crying together in the chair.

Just then, Peter heard the ambulance and glanced up to see the men and women rushing in to help.

"Oh! Sorry!" said the driver. "Traffic! So, sorry!"

"Look what we have here!" said the other ambulance attendant, walking over, cooing over both babies.

Gerald became father to Cassandra's and his baby, and godfather to Lawanda's baby. Oliver bunked with Henry; Cassandra, Gerald, and their baby slept in Peter's bedroom, which they took over immediately. Lawanda and her baby got Oliver's room; and Peter got Cassandra's room. He now had a pink dresser and curtains. It was all temporary, he told himself.

Peter slogged through each day, fatigued and pushing on, now mostly supporting a lot of people. Henry and Oliver had part-time jobs, thank goodness! Henry was almost off to university, but he had decided to stay at home and save money.

Peter looked at his watch. The babies were crying, and everybody was shouting. He'd had a hard day.

"I'm going to the pub," he said, grabbing the novel that he had been re-reading, as he often fell asleep just after opening it up.

He sat by the fire in the pub. The chair was comfortable. He opened his book and promptly nodded off.

"Hello," said a voice.

Peter looked up. It was Helen. He slammed his book closed and jumped up, offering her his chair.

"That's fine, Peter. I can sit over here," she said.

They talked and laughed at Peter's most recent saga. They were friends now, often meeting in the pub after her work. Definitely friends.

CALM ACCEPTANCE

Months later, on a rainy afternoon, with two babies asleep in bassinets near Peter, a sleepy whimper the only sound, Peter rocked them and wondered about the unpredictability of life. Never in his life would he have imagined this scenario at this time in his life. Any dreams of moving to Hampstead were gone, not to mention his travel fantasies. As for Susan–probably still afraid of commitment after their amazing coupling–it seemed like she had faded away into that place where old friends almost disappear. Apparently, the last thing she wanted to be around were crying babies with sticky fingers clutching her newly ironed blouse.

Peter began to notice that his usual high spirit and belief that he could conquer the world had diminished into a calm acceptance that whatever life set in front of him would be dealt with in its own way. That was where freedom lay, he mused, in choosing how to deal with the inevitable.

Angela and Michael had gone to Italy, despite Peter's protestations. Surely, they would get robbed! Surely, they might rather go to France. But, no! They had a clear message from the horoscopes that their visit to Rome and Florence was where they needed to be.

Peter sighed and rocked the bassinet of one baby who threatened to wake up. Each bassinet was armed with a baby bottle lying alongside the baby, within reach of a clinging baby hand.

Peter only wished he was in Rome or Paris or Oslo or New York or Brattleboro.

THE PUB

As Peter sat babysitting the babies again, he pondered the news that the tenants in Brattleboro were moving after years of living there. Peter had hardly noticed its existence anymore, apart from the rental income. Catherine had left the property to him and had confided to him that she felt Peter was her child, in her own mind. After all, Peter realized, she never knew that David was, in fact, not even Peter's father. It took Peter a while to appreciate her story. He didn't mind being a landlord now, though he would have to decide whether he should sell it or look for new tenants. Should he try to go there, too?

Just then, the front door opened quietly, and he heard the young mothers giggling. What a lovely sound to Peter. He was now off duty!

"Hello, Dad," said Cassandra.

"Hello, Dad," said Gerald.

"Hello, Dad," echoed Lawanda.

Peter felt very old at that moment, as he mentally noted that, in fact, he was, "Grandpa."

"Hello, you lot. Giving me my freedom at last?" he said.

"It's all right for you, Dad!" said Cassandra.

"I'm off to the pub, then," said Peter, willing to go out anywhere and feel like a normal person. Perhaps he should call Susan or Helen for a drink. Helen might go for a tomato juice like she often did. It was a bit late. Maybe he'd go alone.

He donned his coat, hat, and umbrella, and decided he'd drive.

"Cheerio, then!" he said.

"Shhh!" they all shushed.

He drove to the pub, parked, and sat in the car for a while. Then he approached the door, the laughter, the warmth. He opened the door and looked in, scanning the customers, jolting a little as he saw Susan with a man whom Peter had never seen before. Should he go in?

It was her right, wasn't it? After all, it had been months since they had parted. He pushed the door open, ambled past her, nodded, and continued towards the bar. She smiled and nodded back. He ordered half a pint and perched himself on a bar stool. No. He didn't have time to chase women. He knocked it back, then left without saying a word, hiding his feelings for the loss of her warmth.

MICHELANGELO'S DAVID

From Cellini's new studio in Florence, he made his way over to the Piazza della Signoria and stopped. As he approached the enormous statue of David carved in white marble by Michelangelo, he was astonished, yet again, at its beauty.

Cellini circled slowly around the most beautiful piece of poetic art he'd ever seen, and he thought about his own idea of a bronze statue of Perseus. It was just like that flash, like that moment as a child, when he had imagined his twelve cups sparkling in the sunlight, yet to be born. Michelangelo, this giant Italian artist and sculptor, was twenty-five years older than Cellini, and was Cellini's hero, beyond even the sculptors of the ancient Greeks.

Cellini studied the muscles in David's thighs and calves. How did Michelangelo do that? Cellini reached up and put his large rough left palm on the calf of David's leg, caressing its smooth marble and its extraordinarily accurate musculature. Cellini looked up and delved into the shape of David's ear, so far above him. That ear! Surely, he'd seen that ear in the older man who always modeled for him. Come to think of it, as Cellini stared at the statute's nose, it was the same silhouette of this same model. Cellini felt two things: one, a surge of pride that his eyes had worked from the real ear and nose of the same model as

Michelangelo's; and two, Cellini was jealous as he took in the genius of Michelangelo, who had so changed the face of art and beauty.

Cellini's mind was a jumble. He hated it when his precious silver cups nudged back into his consciousness. He had been so young and full of energy and enthusiasm back then. And he knew they were still some-where–somewhere. Cellini looked at the eyes of the statue of David, sculpted from a model so young, and then squinted at the older eyes looking just like his own model, yet so many years on. Cellini felt the marble, caressed it again, and imagined how Michelangelo had brought it to life. Cellini would definitely create a masterpiece in bronze, hope-fully comparable to Michelangelo's great genius. Cellini knew that he, himself, was also a genius, if only younger and still full of the bravado, that–if Michelangelo ever had it–was likely waning in Michelangelo's older years.

Cellini frowned, as his active mind traveled back to the moment his cups had been stolen. As long as he lived, he knew he would never forget the devastation, humiliation, and anger he'd felt. His curse of bad luck would endure for however long it would take for his cups to be returned to Florence, even if they surfaced long after Cellini's own demise.

A Magnet in his Mind

Peter thought the wisest move for him was to take a break. He asked the higher-ups and was informed that he had accrued three weeks' paid holiday.

Peter knew it was a long time, and he had only traveled to the continent in the past. He envisioned the USA, and then Japan and perhaps Vietnam. But there were also Brazil and Cuba and Guatemala.

Yet Italy pushed her antique face again and again into the forefront of his mind. Her antiquity was even more appealing than the Mayan ruins. He had heard it was very hot and sweaty in South America and Mexico anyway, and even though Rome would be very hot, it would be dry—and there would be air conditioning. Ah! That felt tolerable. Enjoyable. Then there was Venice, as well—gondolas and tiny arched foot bridges—the water levels rising, the city sinking. Perhaps he should go there before it sank too far, and the residents and vendors might have to leave for higher grounds, and the tourists might have to be turned away.

Peter remembered that the silver cups were in an Italian museum now in Florence, probably behind thick glass. Yes, he had read that in the newspaper when Catherine had returned them to the Carabinieri Art Squad while they stood at her hotel door and waited for her to hand them over. Perhaps they would not be shown at all. They were a magnet

163

in his mind, those silver cups! The Cellini silver cups! They seemed to be an echo in his brain, and the Amazon disappeared, the Yangtze River faded away, and the Balinese dancers smiled and waved goodbye.

The cups were seductive, even though Peter knew in his very bones that in some way they could be a danger to him. And yet, they were a part of the family history, like old friends that had made up his family saga, making him into a detective and even finding his own father for him. Or the father had become his father, because Peter was a detective and had followed the story of his so-called "uncle," until the shocking moment when he compared his DNA with David's and Michael's.

But before this possible trip, Peter again thought that he really ought to see a therapist to help him sort out the seeming contradiction that was certainly responsible for his unspoken anger–mostly for Angela. Although the family members were all smiles and toasts, it wasn't so happily ever after and it niggled Peter to the core. He found that his anger at Angela was deep. His fists still showed him his deep, unconscious fury at her.

He tried to forgive her for keeping silent all his youthful years about who his real father was, but like a song that kept surfacing in his brain, his anger at her rose often enough like a whale in the ocean, showing its barnacled head.

Peter felt he was the epitome of the stony-faced British man, not showing his true feelings or bothering people with his own petty trage-dies. He'd seen so much worse–right there in Rottingdean. He hardly felt his story worth a moment's notice, and he was not about to confide in anyone in town. So, he'd found a therapist in London, far from the notice of anyone he knew.

This time it was a man, rather withered, and full of experience and wisdom, with white sideburns, a full head of pure white hair, a grey mus-tache and rather informal attire.

"Come in, Mr. Evans," said Dr. Friedman.

Peter sat down in the obvious chair. He checked the paintings around the walls and could see Freudian meanings right away. He didn't feel particularly sexy and had not really felt that way for years. Well, perhaps a little. But it was not what he had booked this appointment with this elderly, wise man for. Peter just wanted to deal with his anger about his mother.

"Why do you call her Angela?" asked the therapist.

"Pardon?"

"Do you call her Mother?"

Peter flinched. It was a perfectly simple question that he had heard all his life. But it made him angry. He almost up and left, right then and there. He felt that this was about anger, not about names!

"I don't know, really," he replied. Peter studied Dr. Friedman's posture, the way he leaned back and showed his shiny black laced shoes. He imagined his wife polishing them for him. Peter felt a little superior, as he had always polished his own shoes.

"I always heard people call her Angela, so I just copied them. I don't really know how it happened."

"Do you love her?"

"Pardon?"

"Do you love your mother?"

Love her? For Heaven's sake. What business of his was it? Love had nothing to do with it! He wondered why he was suddenly so angry at these perfectly innocent questions. He remembered his months of therapy with Helen. She had taught him so much. He remembered going through these very questions with her. He had forgotten.

"You know," said Peter, leaning forward, "I am so sorry, but I think I've made a mistake."

What really irritated Peter was the therapist's mustache. It was too long. Peter could only imagine food stuck to it, just wiped away before Peter entered the dungeon.

But he smiled, as was expected. His mother had nothing to do with it. It was clearly all Jeannie's fault, or his father's. After all, Peter had been abandoned. What was worse than that? Now that he'd realized that, he felt he could leave–just get up, shake hands, and leave. Yes, leaving was a very lovely prospect, in that moment. However, it was true, getting there in the storm had been very uncomfortable, and if he left now, he would have to get home in this windy, wet weather, and perhaps catch pneumonia.

"I almost always called her Angela," he said.

"Do you remember calling her 'Mother' ever?"

Was there something wrong with this man's hearing? Didn't he just say he always called her Angela? He hated himself just now. His anger had clearly transferred to the therapist–poor man. Just doing his job.

"No," Peter started, his tone rather defensive. "Well, now I think about it, I called her Mum sometimes." And, since he was talking to a therapist, Peter felt no guilt at being blunt in reaction to this persistent question.

Peter realized he was being overly reactive, and he tried, as he shifted back in his chair, to figure out what his problem was. But then he realized he was paying this man to figure it out for him. Peter was impatient. He realized he had learned so much from his sessions with Helen that he wished this man could just continue with her questions already answered and move straight on to the final answer.

Peter stood up. He cleared his throat. Dr. Friedman's mouth fell open.

"I am so sorry, Dr. Friedman, but I think I have made a mistake here. I realize I have already gone through a great deal of therapy with my first therapist, and I don't think this is what I actually need right now. Sorry, but I really must go."

He stood up, reached out, shook the doctor's hand, and walked right out the door. He felt a great deal of jubilation and daring for leaving before the session had finished. It was better than a trip abroad. As he stepped outside, he noticed that the rain had stopped and now there was an entirely new cast–fresh, brisk, with windy air–and he realized that he loved his life. There was nothing wrong with him, for heaven's sake! In fact, perhaps it was the doctor that needed attention.

Peter ran to the tube station, but stopped short on the way, wondering if he might just stop a while, and have a nice hot pot of tea at one of the local cafés.

RELIEF

Later that day, back in Rottingdean, as Peter was just parking the car to go shopping, he spotted Susan walking up the street, arm-in-arm with a rather handsome man. Peter was devastated yet again–all his persistent dreams gone in one second flat. He ducked down in his car, hoping she wouldn't see him. But here they came. Peter opened the window on the passenger side of the car.

"Well, hello!" he bellowed in too friendly a manner.

"Peter! How lovely to see you!" said Susan. Lovely, my hat, thought Peter. And who is the charming man on your arm?

"This is my brother, John. John, this is Peter."

Peter turned quite red and reached out of the window with a hearty hand, gesturing towards this handsome chap.

"Happy to meet you," said John. "Susan can't stop talking about you!"

Peter's ears were so red now that he feared they might just drop off his head.

"Susan has talked about you, as well," Peter lied. Had she? He couldn't really remember. They had only talked on the phone a few times in the past months. But at least she didn't contradict him. Perhaps she couldn't remember, anyway. One could hope.

"We were just going to have a spot of tea," said John. "Perhaps you would care to join us?"

"I was just imaging a cup of tea and scones. I would be delighted."

Peter straightened out the car in the parking space, got out, slammed the door, and joined the two, with Susan in the middle, all arms linked.

Susan and John seemed to have a certain café in mind, so Peter strode along with them, all of them getting wet in the sprinkle, and all of them deeply breathing in the cold air.

Peter felt a sense of relief because he might actually make a new male friend for life–if things worked out–and he was thrilled that he had left the therapist and returned to Rottingdean, just in time to meet Susan by chance, and perhaps, change the course of his life with her.

SUSAN'S MOTHER

With Michael and Angela nearby, and Susan needing him now, as he did her—and of course, with Cassandra, Lawanda and the babies—well, it looked like his lingering old Hampstead dream might never happen.

He still took the train to London at least twice a week for his job, so he didn't lose touch with the big city.

Tonight, a month after he had run into Helen, he would embrace Susan. It had been months since her son had died. Peter was sensitive to her need to be in mourning. He felt a need for physical warmth. Babies were cuddly, but not the same as a woman. He needed to put his arms around Susan and squeeze her until she purred. But, of course, he only dreamed of that.

They agreed to meet again at her place soon. The squeezing part might have to wait. It might also have to wait until Susan's mum went upstairs to bed. He hoped her mother was tired! Her brother had apparently gone back to London.

His mobile phone buzzed.

"Hello?"

"It's Mum!" sobbed Susan.

"I'll be right there," Peter said. He enjoyed the fact that no remarks had to be politely made now.

Susan opened the door and gestured for him to come inside. Once the door was closed, he opened his arms, and she fell into them, hugging her gently–very gently. Her hair smelled of some divine shampoo. Or was it a delicate perfume? He pulled in the scent and did not want to let her go. He wanted to kiss her patiently, then devour her, throw her on the floor and ravish her.

But then she broke away with a teary face and said, "Come in. I'll make tea, but first you should see Mum."

"Of course," he said, like a man who had no thoughts of sex on his mind.

He climbed the stairs and went into her mother's room. The old woman lay there, her breathing labored, her eyes closed. The room smelled dank, old, like bad body odor.

"I am very worried that she might have pneumonia. She's having trouble breathing. Maybe we should we take her to the hospital?" Susan asked, arriving with a mug of tea.

"Not yet. Why not call in Dr. Pickford–he isn't far away," said Peter who was glad that even though doctors hardly made home visits anymore, their old family doctor in Rottingdean still made them.

Peter thought of Susan's arms, her legs, her smile. He couldn't have cared less about her mother or the old doctor.

"Ask him if he can come right away."

Susan's mum had been a quiet presence when Peter had come round for tea in the past. He felt embarrassed at the echo in his brain: let her die, for heaven's sake! I need this wonderful woman all to myself.

Susan called the doctor, who promised to come by within the hour.

Peter frowned. An hour?

"More tea?" said Susan.

"Of course," he said, wanting to give her the sympathy that might accompany it.

The electric kettle boiled rapidly, and the teapot was heated. Susan had hers in a mug, too. It comforted them, no matter what container they drank it from.

"Susan," Peter started. He reached his hand over and put it on top of hers. She looked at him with large eyes, her mouth slightly parted. Was that a longing for him; perhaps she was wishing that her mum wasn't there and that the doctor wasn't arriving?

"Oh, Peter!" she said.

"Susan," he replied. No more words were necessary. One day it would happen. Just not today.

The doctor arrived and was taken upstairs to do the usual tests.

"She ought to go to hospital right away," he concluded. "She has pneumonia. I think you could make it by car, but I recommend going right away."

"Thank you, Dr. Pickford. I'll call ahead."

"I'll dress her," said Susan.

Peter escorted the doctor to the door and thanked him.

"How's your mother, then, Peter?"

"Doing well, thank you. Walks every day!" answered Peter, closing the door gently, glad Angela was still just fine.

SEXUAL DESIRE

How long does it take to know when to move closer without ruining a perfectly good friendship?

Some weeks later, after Susan's mother had died in her sleep at the hospital, Peter arrived at Susan's door. He straightened his tie, which was always loose, and brushed back his hair, which was always falling into his eyes. He'd get a haircut in the morning.

Just as he was going to knock, the door opened, and he saw the most beautiful face in the world, with red eyes and wet cheeks and a clear ability to love so hard that the risk of loss was worth it. Her mother and her son—gone within a few months of each other. Only her memories were left—like they were still alive, yet, of course, clearly only in her head.

Peter gathered her into his arms, and she cried on his shoulder. He held her close and waited only for her signal that it was time to part. She held him for so long he felt a little embarrassed. Was he that important to her? Or was she just devastated, and would calm down and be her usual reserved self in a few minutes? Peter held her, and then kissed her forehead, her cheeks, and her nose. After a pause, as he looked at her devastated face, he planted a soft kiss upon her open mouth. He waited forever for her response. She kissed him back with surprising passion. Peter was not sure he was ready for it, as this beautiful kiss was a little

173

out of character. He pushed her gently away and looked into her eyes to get a better sense of her feelings.

"Sorry, sorry!" she spluttered.

He pulled her back into his embrace, kissed her all over her face and then back to her inviting and expectant lips. A good line had been crossed.

"Oh, dear! Do come in," she said, opening the door wide.

Peter stepped into her warm house, and she closed the door. She showed him into the living room and gestured towards the couch. The curtains were closed, and the fire was lit. Peter glanced at the comforta-ble-looking chair near the fire but understood that a couch had greater possibilities. As he sat down, he reached out his hand and pulled her close to him to kiss her. She leaned towards him as he softly guided her lips to his. He could tell her position was very awkward, so he pulled her down to sit next to him, and their arms wrapped around each other as they laughed, rolled off the couch and onto the rug.

Peter felt a surge of sexual desire that, he realized, he had been hold-ing back for years. She was so responsive that he put his hand under her cardigan and moved it around to the back of her bra. Then he slid his hand underneath it to her bare breast. There was no child to tend to and no mother to consider. It was finally a time and place where love and lust could flourish. Peter was bursting with passion after so long a time, yet he still felt he had to hold back until he felt a hundred percent will-ingness coming from her. She reached under her cardigan and moved his hand to cup her full breast. Peter felt the green light sparkle, and his passion opened up with full force. At last, the possibilities of oneness filled his body. It had been so long!

MOURNING

"...my freedom," Susan mumbled, rolling away on the floor from Peter, whose eyes were still shut from the aftereffects of their glorious coupling.

"What? Sorry?" Peter spluttered, pulling up his trousers.

"Peter, dear. It's too soon. That was lovely, but right now, it's all too much for me. Winston and now my mother–just so soon," she sniffed and then burst out crying.

"I'm sorry, my love," Peter said, cradling her as she cried into his shoulder.

"No," she said, "I'm the one who's sorry. No, not about this. This was a dream. It's just that I can't do this right now. I'm in mourning for the loves of my life," she said, blowing her nose and dabbing her eyes. "Sorry, sorry!" she said.

Mourning was that state of being Peter understood only too well. Her sadness brought up his own suppressed, deep, and confused feelings about Jeannie. But that was so long ago. He was ready now. But, as he swallowed, his throat pinching, he knew he had to understand. No, he really understood. *She has her own agenda* floated through his brain.

"Come, my love," he said, standing up and helping her up. They stood embracing, and he realized that this was a precious moment that would become the past, and that further comfort was in no way guaranteed.

Peter gently held her away from him, leaned forward, kissed her lips lightly and said, "Would you mind if I go now?"

"Please, Peter. Forgive me. I can't help it."

He took that as an affirmative, grabbed his coat, and walked to the door like someone was pushing him out of her house. He glanced back at Susan, standing like a helpless rag doll, her head down, arms hanging like weights by her sides, and not a hint of reluctance to see him going.

Peter walked out and closed the door. He was tired and sad. One moment he had been a happy man, ready for a bright future, and the next, he was the same sad man with no clear future with the woman he loved. He loved Susan. He also understood she needed that in-between time to shore up a balance between the past and the present, the dying and the living, misery and hope.

Peter walked home, his lungs filling with fresh ocean air, and he picked up his stride. They were a perfect match. He felt it so deeply that he knew she must feel it, too. It just wasn't the right time, was it?

He reached his front door and pulled it open, wondering if the right time would ever come. Perhaps, he mused, there was never a right time for anything.

Back in the kitchen, he sat down, and, for once, he didn't even glance at the kettle. Tea would not heal this. He had to wait. But how long? How long until the time was right? He looked at his watch, as if it could give him the answer, and realized he was desperately lonely. The quiet was overbearing. He left the house and drove to the pub and ordered a large beer, gulping it down as if it would help. People around him were arguing heartily about politics. Even a whole beer was not working. He sat with his loneliness and asked himself—what is my agenda?

NEW ADVENTURE

It took Peter a long time to understand what love truly was. He thought about Jeannie, whom he had deeply loved, to whom he had given his very soul. His head fell forward as he sat there in his favorite chair; the ocean view blocked by fog. He remembered that, in the end, he didn't love her. Wasn't love supposed to be forever? Apparently not. He had failed with Jeannie.

Then he sat up straight and saw the ocean showing itself between clouds of fog and realized that, indeed, Jeannie must have once loved him well, and must have stopped loving him. Otherwise, she could never have wanted to push him over the cliff. Peter was devastated to see how their love had not only faded away but had become a negative in their lives—a wish for each other's demise.

Now Peter realized he loved Susan. But he had also felt that for Helen. Perhaps this wasn't as deep a love as one feels when young. Yes, that was it. But his children were now the love of his life, and his grandchild was so close to his heart that he was astounded. Imagine, he thought, that he had not wanted Cassandra to have it! But logically, he could see that, if it had never been born, he probably just wouldn't have experienced this new love until later.

Oliver and Henry were wonderful. Well, Oliver was still shouting out the embarrassing truth, and was annoying that way. But, in another way, Peter felt it was endearing and lovable. Cassandra! Now, Cassandra was difficult, disobedient, ornery and a bit rude. But perhaps he secretly loved her the most. He loved her in the way he loved his own slightly off-kilter ways that had made him a good detective. He loved how she encouraged him to play his penny whistle. Nobody else ever seemed to notice he'd played. Yes, somehow, Cassandra was like him in ways he understood, perhaps in ways nobody else, even Gerald, might understand.

Yes, he loved Henry's caring ways, and Oliver's big mouth. Yet he couldn't fathom how all three of his children, from the same parents, were so different from each other. He loved them beyond anything he could have ever imagined.

Peter felt older these days. White hairs were hiding in his otherwise young, fair sideburns. Perhaps he was tired. Perhaps the idea of retirement was periodically at the forefront of his mind–yes, some years off– but now almost within sight.

Hampstead still called in a faint voice. Helen and Susan were here in Rottingdean, rooted, or perhaps stuck in their ways, so they possibly wouldn't ever want to move away. Anyway, these days, Susan seemed otherwise occupied!

Peter yearned to be unstuck. Yet, he couldn't imagine how to be that way, how he could move away and not cuddle his grandchild and watch him grow. And yet–and yet.

Peter leapt up, grabbed his umbrella and raincoat, wrote a short note to the family, and left the house. He drove the car to the seaside, parked, and strode over to the bus stop. Four easy miles and he could be at the Brighton train station. He jumped onto the bus, sat down and looked out the window, noticing the sleepy sheep and the chewing cows on one side, and the rumbling ocean on the other. He peered at the horizon, now cleared of fog, and imagined he could just see Italy. Bright sparkles grew in his eyes, and he knew now where he was headed. No suitcase, no ticket. Just as he was, he was off to a new adventure. He thought of the silver cups.

FREEDOM

Peter jumped on the train headed from Brighton to London, and once in London, he rushed along with the usual frantic crowd, then changed to another train going to Italy via France.

Peter smiled a wicked smile to himself. He had no toothbrush and no passport, but he had his new credit card. Freedom surged through his veins. The further he got away from his children and the babies, the lighter he felt. But he was alarmed at the magnetic attraction pulling him to Italy, for just one more look at the silver cups. He'd read in *The Times* that they were on full display with a guard and thick glass to protect them. They were like an old love he could not shake off. He pondered his theory about bad luck and the cups. Well, after all, they were finally back in Italy where they belonged, the country where Cellini had finished them so lovingly back in 1527.

Peter traveled in a sort of daze, dozing off with a smile. The country-side flew by. The people around him spoke French, then Italian, and sprinklings of German. He lived on strange snacks that were wheeled by on a tea trolly, and tea and coffee that tasted, at the least, suspicious.

After what seemed to be three days, he finally got off the train in Florence, his suit quite rumpled and his beard rough. Hailing a taxi, he headed straight to the Silver Museum at the Palazzo Pitti. He thought of calling his family but decided against it. His quick note would have to do.

It was hot outside, then cool in the museum. He was too tired to look around and only had one desire.

"Excuse me, but where are the Cellini cups?"

A bored guard pointed him towards the next room where the cups were displayed.

Small and precious—there they were—behind a very thick glass case on a sturdy pedestal. Peter stood rather near them, imagining all the stories he'd heard about them. He thought of Cellini, dead for hundreds of years, who probably never knew what had happened to his amazing cups.

The guard inched closer to Peter and leaned in slightly. Peter glanced at him and stepped away from the thick glass, smiling sheepishly. The guard stepped back.

Peter wiped the back of his hand on his rough chin, looked down, and noticed his crumpled suit. Perhaps he looked suspicious, especially with the hot, smelly sweat pouring from under Peter's arms. That might have been a giveaway to the guard. Peter's Italian was no good, so he didn't say anything to him.

Peter stood there for a while, circling the case that stood centrally in the high-ceilinged room with its marble floor. A photo would be wonderful, but somehow Peter could not become that kind of tourist. Perhaps, anyway, it might be against the rules. He would check to see if they sold postcards of the cups.

As he stared at the cups, Peter remembered the six cups that Catherine's helper, Christopher, had dug up at Angela's house. He remembered that he had heard that she'd had to give them to the police at her London hotel. He remembered that the cups had been tarnished then, not shiny, like these polished ones in front of him.

As he stood there, staring at the twelve tiny cups, Peter imagined what might have happened: Cellini, riding his horse, the cups being stolen, a fight, a theft, a secret sale at the wharf, a crash of a ship in Cornwall, a little girl playing with them, a fire and her death, a train ride up to Portobello Market in London and then his father and uncle, as teenagers, buying them from the rag-and-bone man. He shrugged. It was just his imagination, after all. Where did he come up with this story? It must have been from reading David's manuscript–except, of course, the bit about the rag-and-bone man, and David and Michael buying them from him; their fight over them; the accidental death of David; the jailing of Catherine all those years; the redemption of Michael, and the truth from Angela about Peter's real father, with his DNA as final proof. It was a torrent of memories that flashed through his mind, in only that brief moment between a glance at the guard and a final hard look at the silver cups.

Peter stepped back, bidding a silent farewell to those sparkling Cellini cups. He purchased several postcards with pictures of the silver cups, and then, after a slight pause, looking at his train ticket back to London in his sweaty palm, he was strangely ready for an immediate flight home. After a hot shower and shave, he would feel ready to hold as many babies as life required of him, with a feeling of confidence that, now, all would be well.

TIME

Once at home in Rottingdean, Peter had been reassured at seeing the cups firmly ensconced back in Italy, and yet, however much Peter loved babies, their crying was disturbing his usual composure. The night cries were the worst as he woke up immediately several times a night, thanking God that he wasn't the one who had to comfort them. And one baby often woke the other one up and it went on just long enough to thoroughly wake Peter. He struggled off to work each day, yawning, after drinking two cups of strong morning coffee.

Quite often, Peter felt in the way of Gerald, Henry, Lawanda, and Cassandra–and even Oliver–while he yawned incessantly. Again, it occurred to him it might be time to quietly take up residence in Hampstead. He had invited Susan for dinner after he'd returned from Italy, and since then, she and he were getting quite close again. That man from the pub was apparently long gone. It had been months now. Would she come with him? Would Michael give him the flat?

Surely it was time. Cassandra hardly had time to speak with him unless she was asking him to hold the baby. And Lawanda was up and out to the baby minder's before the sun came up so she could dash to her own job. There was no peace and no time to sit back and contemplate–Peter's favorite way to be in life. He'd raised three children already, and he admitted to himself that, at times, he was truly fed up with it all.

"Can I borrow the car, Dad?" shouted Oliver down the hallway.

"Of course. Be careful! I'll walk down–it'll do me good."

"Cheerio, Dad. See you later!" shouted Oliver, as he started to race out the door. Henry dashed into the kitchen.

"Tea's ready," said Peter.

"Ta, Dad. Must run!" Henry slurped his tea and put his cup down in the sink. "Sorry!" he said, rushing down the hallway.

Peter felt like a rock and anchor that everybody circled around in their mad dash to cope with not enough time in the day. He sighed. It was definitely time to move on. He liked being helpful, but he didn't like the constant interruptions, and he didn't like the feeling that he might be getting old. It seemed, even years ago with his own three children, that nobody had been constantly rushing around, beating deadlines, like they had to these days.

Peter picked up *The Times*, which he now had delivered every morning, and sat back sipping tea and trying to relax like a normal person.

Gerald pushed the kitchen door open.

"Tea?" said Peter. "Sorry, coffee's ready, as well."

"Thanks. Any good news?" Gerald asked, nodding at Peter's newspaper.

"Never!" said Peter. "They don't print good news. Ever!"

"Cheers!" said Gerald, knocking back his hastily poured cup of coffee. He grabbed his coat while shouldering the baby carrier with his sleeping baby aboard, rocking it automatically back and forth.

"I'm late for Angela's!" he said in a stage whisper, hustling along to the front door.

"As usual," muttered Peter, holding the paper up again. "Cheerio, then!"

Peter knew there was a gigantic pile of laundry by the washing machine. He couldn't help himself: he put his paper on the table, downed the dregs in his tea, stood up like a soldier, walked over to the pile, heaved it up and, like a robot, stuffed it into the washing machine.

"Is this what my life has come to?" he muttered to himself. He tossed in the detergent and pressed the buttons. The washing machine was a constant noise in the house now. He realized he actually just couldn't stand it anymore, even if he was the one who had turned it on.

It was now time for coffee. He poured his small, special one cup of coffee, tried to block out the mechanical noise coming from the washing machine, and sat back down to finish the paper. He would work from home today.

Yes, he thought, time to move on, yet—he couldn't help it—he phoned Susan and they agreed to meet up again at the usual café.

TRANSLATE

Later that week, Peter mused how his life had revolved around the kitchen—how the sitting room, with its large picture window and its view of the endless ocean, was mostly reserved for company. It was just too far down the hallway from the jolly teakettle and the warmth that a cup of tea promised. When Peter thought about it, he didn't really like tea, and yet he felt it was rather like the protein of his life, and the reason to get out of bed and face whatever challenges lay ahead that day. His afternoon tea was the one that he felt he deserved. He was lucky if anyone brought it to him with a giving gesture and a smile. With that hot, sweet taste, he could settle down for another two hours and accept the rhythm of life that these cups of tea amounted to. In fact, he could not even imagine a single afternoon without that pause, that moment of comfort where he'd take a sip, then sit back and say, "Ahh!" He only added half a teaspoon of sugar, and that sweet taste, right at the last sip, was perhaps, what he treasured the most. The warm teapot, huddling under its tea cozy, knitted with love by his mother, was what it was really all about. It meant home and satisfaction, no matter what time of day.

This gray day, promising rain, was begging for that little pot of good, black English tea, to be boiled and settled, then poured into his cup, while he added a few chocolate biscuits to his side dish.

There was a knock at the door, and in walked Susan. Did this subtle, friendly intrusion mean they were truly moving towards being a permanent couple?

"Ahh! Hello Susan! Just in time for tea!"

Peter glanced at his one-person teapot, walked down the hallway to the front door and helped her off with her coat, then said, "You look lovely!"

Susan straightened her hair, glanced down at her blue dress, and smiled at Peter. "A cup of tea would answer my prayers!"

They walked into the warm kitchen and sat together, alone for once.

Peter immediately took down the larger teapot and filled it with hot water, then turned the kettle back on.

"Susan," Peter said, "Is there something wrong?"

"Let's have a cuppa first, then I'll tell you everything."

Peter rustled around and fussed over the preparation of her tea. He was delighted to have an equal partner to share teatime with–for once.

"I have to move house," Susan blurted out after her first sip. "The landlord is selling up. We've been there for years. I almost began to think I'd be there until I died."

"Oh, Susan! I am so sorry to hear this!" In fact, Peter was rather pleased to hear it. Perhaps it was the beginning of his dream. His mind hovered over his idea of Hampstead, even though he'd mostly given that up since he had become a grandfather. His house here in Rottingdean was too small to add an additional person, even if she shared Peter's bed. Peter looked at Susan and imagined her waking him up in the morning with a kiss. What a dream!

"You can move in here for a while," he said, mentally slapping his hand for saying this without a plan laid out. But it seemed the only way.

"Oh, Peter! How sweet! But I have all my furniture and endless things I've collected over the years. You all are overflowing here, if I may say so, with prams and toys and babies and people. I really must find a place of my own." She looked at him with a message in her eyes that Peter was desperately trying to translate.

YOU CAN'T LEAVE NOW

"I'm leaving Rottingdean," announced Lawanda the next week.

"You're what?" said Peter, rocking Lawanda's baby.

"I've got a job in London, thanks to you, of course, so I will have to move there right away."

"London?" protested Cassandra. "You can't leave now!"

"I forbid it!" said Henry.

"Who will my baby cry with?" kidded Gerald.

"I know, it's true. You all have been so generous and wonderful. You are family to me. But I have found my distant aunt, a widow, living in London who can take us in, and it's only a short distance from my new job. I have to do it!"

Lawanda and Cassandra looked hard at each other, as many unsaid and loving words passed between them.

"Our babies are like twins!" protested Cassandra.

Peter felt like his own daughter was leaving as he nursed an ache in his heart. Right after that, he realized there would be fewer people queue-ing for the bathroom sink, so he was ashamed of being a little relieved—not to mention the slight strain on their finances for the past year.

But he so loved his new grandchildren. Losing one was going to be hard. He kissed the baby's forehead.

"I shall miss you, my darling," he said, rocking and hugging the bright-eyed baby.

"Who will look after the baby?" he asked Lawanda.

"My aunt's daughter has children, and they are at home, so that will work out just fine. I hope you will all come and visit."

"You must visit regularly, too. They need each other!" said Cassandra.

Just then both babies started crying, like they knew something was wrong. Perhaps they understood what everybody was saying? Gerald held his baby, as he and Peter rocked and cooed the babies, until they calmed down.

The rain pelted down, beating against the windowpanes, and the wind howled. Peter gave the baby to Lawanda and, without thinking, switched the kettle back on.

Peter pulled out his handkerchief and found himself silently weeping. It wasn't like him! But the contrast between his love of these two new family members, and his relief at their coming departure, and his coming ability to get into the bathroom, was too much. He'd grown so very fond of both. He would have loved to put his hand out and say, "No! No! You must stay here!" But that would have been impractical and impossible. He realized that all his children would also be departing soon enough, as was natural. They had their lives to live. He had his to live, too. He'd almost forgotten what that was all about. But it was clear–the big transition was coming.

VICTORIA AND ALBERT MUSEUM

A few months later, the table was laid at Peter's house for the whole family, including Michael, Angela, Susan, and Lawanda, who was just arriving at the front door. It was Peter's birthday, and Cassandra had decided it was time for a celebration. It actually felt as if Lawanda had never left, what with the volume of noise provided by only one extra child.

When Lawanda entered the front door, with her contagious smile and her baby, who had her mother's smile, everybody leapt up and went over to them to welcome their old, adopted family. Lawanda and her baby hugged and kissed their first family from England, and then she reached behind her, and dragged in her newly discovered, shy distant cousin.

"Please meet Howard, my new husband."

Hands were clasped, backs were patted, and after a few comments about the sunny weather, "but cold, but cold," they all sat around the long kitchen table, and Cassandra played "mum," pouring their tea from the large teapot.

Peter introduced Susan, who had also just arrived.

"What's going on in London?" Peter asked Lawanda.

"There's an exhibition of the Cellini silver cups," said Lawanda, then sipped her tea. There was a deep silence as everybody looked at Michael and Angela. Michael then started coughing, and Angela patted his back vigorously.

"Not the real Cellini cups?" said Oliver.

"The Cellini cups, of course! What other Cellini cups would there be?" puffed Henry.

Peter studied Michael's face, suddenly red and blotchy. "In London?" he asked, a look of horror upon his face, imagining all of them leaning over and absorbing those Cellini cups.

"Where are they?" asked Michael, shrugging off Angela's back patting.

"Victoria and Albert Museum," said Lawanda, bouncing her baby on her knee, while popping a piece of toast and marmalade into his little, open mouth.

"We have to see them," said Angela.

"Do we?" asked Peter, thinking he'd rather not see them ever again.

"Of course, we do!" said Michael.

"We live near there," said Lawanda. "You must all come to London for tea very soon."

"How about tomorrow?" suggested Michael.

"Sounds lovely," said Lawanda.

Peter groaned. Michael clapped. Everybody's head swiveled towards Peter.

THE CELLINI MANUSCRIPT

As per plan, they all took the train to London and met outside the Victoria and Albert Museum. It was grand inside. The little group wandered along the endless hallways until they came to a giant room with sculptures from Italy. In the very center of the room was an exhibition on a stand, where the glass surrounding it looked like it was an inch thick. A guard hovered nearby.

They wandered in, trying not to look too enthusiastic, and walked over to the exhibition of the troublesome Cellini silver cups.

Michael was clinging to Angela's hand as she gently held him back. Peter and Susan circled the case to see the cups from all sides, taking in the astrological engravings.

"They're beautiful!" said Cassandra.

"Let's steal them!" joked Oliver.

All their eyes shot in Oliver's direction, and they all said, "Shhh!"

The guard became alarmed and strode over to them and hovered, acting like he was grasping an imaginary baton.

"Sorry!" said Oliver.

"Silly idiot!" said Cassandra.

"I think it was funny," said Henry.

"Well, that's enough joking for today, then," said Angela.

Peter pulled Susan around the case, remembering his own disheveled visit to the cups in Italy. The lighting was different now and showed their sparkle off like they had just been polished that day.

Lawanda guided the toddlers around and around. Cassandra put her arm around her, and Lawanda said, "Well, the cups are very beautiful, but I really can't see what all the fuss is about."

Everybody turned towards Lawanda. Peter had no intention of telling her the whole story just yet. After all, this was a kind of farewell to the cups. The museums and their countries could argue over who owned them. Peter was finished with the whole story and wondered how he'd been talked into visiting these cups– the source of his family troubles for as long as he could remember.

Michael put his nose right up to the glass until a foggy mark was forming on it. The guard stepped forward.

"Sorry, mate," said Michael sheepishly to the nervous guard. "Couldn't help it."

"Time for tea!" suggested Lawanda, and they all followed her, Cassandra, and Gerald out of the exhibition hall to find the tearoom.

Henry lingered behind. Peter was wondering what Henry was thinking. He anxiously called to him, "Let's go have a cuppa, then, Henry."

"Just imagining the creator of these jewels–Cellini," said Henry. "I wonder what he was like?"

"There's a manuscript I have to show you written by your great uncle, David."

"You already told me stories about it. Maybe I will go to Italy after I have read it."

Peter frowned. "You've already seen the cups today in London!"

Henry was a sensible lad. But then, so had Peter been, and he'd been drawn into this saga, hardly realizing it had happened. Peter remembered from therapy that he only had control of himself and had no control over others–even over Henry.

"Never mind, Henry. I'll give it to you. Just don't be drawn in. It's bad luck!"

"Dad, I am not superstitious like you, but I do like history. I'd really like to read it now. Where do you keep it?"

Peter massaged his chin. "It's stowed away somewhere. I will have a look tomorrow."

"Dad! You know exactly where it is, right?"

Peter felt a wave of nausea. At some level, he really didn't want to let Henry read it. Perhaps Peter was, indeed, a little superstitious.

"Could be in the attic at Angela's," Peter said.

HOW MUCH?

Peter had done whatever he could do up to now for his family, and he had done what he could do for Lawanda and her baby. With her moving on to London and finding that distant relative who married her, she had satisfied any difficulties with her immigrant status. One less person using the bathroom; one less baby waking him up at night.

The painters had long come and gone. The pictures were back in place, if slightly altered in placement. He loved those pictures like they were a solid part of his history and memories. Their sameness settled him back into his home, where things were of a permanent nature, despite the rest of the world swirling around him.

Susan had settled into her new flat–walking distance from Peter's house–no point in moving in together. She liked her own paintings, but they could share a bed as often as they liked and have a laugh sitting by her own picture window.

Yes, time had moved along, and nothing much bothered him anymore. Work was always an interesting challenge, and he knew he was very good at it. He loved using his highly-developed senses and his expert knowledge, but mostly his suspicious and active mind, figuring out how, when, and why crimes were committed. He was constantly struck by the blind spots people of normal intelligence had of their own lies, exaggerations, and justifications. He actually laughed regularly in aston-ishment at the latest lie someone told about their reasons for committing a crime. Always perfectly understood by the criminal, white collar or not.

"Dad?" said Cassandra.

"Yes, my love, sorry, back in my own mind again."

"You're always doing that. I'm used to it," she said. "Oh, yes. We're going out tonight and wondered…."

"Of course!" Peter said. He didn't mind a bit. He had a good mystery to finish, and it would be fine.

"He'll be fast sleep by the time we leave, not to worry!"

"I'm not worried, you know that!"

In fact, he rather wished he could take over earlier so he could rock the baby to sleep and kiss his warm forehead. He'd look in once an hour and place his hand on the little bundle anyway.

"Dad?"

"Yes?"

"We found a flat."

"Jolly good," said Peter, who had forgotten they were looking for one. "Where is it?"

"Rottingdean, of course!"

"So, I can still babysit for you?"

"That's the idea!" she said, planting a kiss on his cheek.

Peter was relieved that they were leaving and delighted that they were staying local, yet still wondering when he might make his escape to Hampstead.

"I'll help you move, just let me know what you need."

"Money might help a lot!" she laughed.

"Love you, my dear! Whatever you need!" Peter fumbled in his pocket and brought out his wallet for some cash.

"Can you possibly write us a check, Dad?"

"Oh! How much do you need?"

"A lot to move in, I'm afraid. We have savings, but not really enough."

Peter got up, went to his desk, pulled out his checkbook and said, "How much is a lot?"

"A lot, a lot!" she said.

He wrote a large sum so that they could keep their meager savings and handed it to her.

"Love you so much, Dad! Gerald will be relieved!"

"Love you all!" said Peter. "Glad you're staying in Rottingdean!"

SIR FREDERICK BURROWS

One day, a month or so later, after the big move, Cassandra wandered into the house to retrieve her cardigan. Peter looked up, not unhappy on this bleak day, to see her smiling face so soon.

"Dad! You look sad!"

"Rubbish!" Peter exclaimed, making an effort to look pleasant.

"No, but really, Dad. You should be relieved that we've all gone. This winter you'll have the fireplace all to yourself."

"Well, that'll be a relief!" he joked.

"I mean, we're only around the corner. Anyway, can you babysit tomorrow night?"

"Here or there?"

"There, of course. "

"Is there room for me to sit down yet?"

"By then, there will be your old chair in front of our telly."

"Then, I will!"

"Bye, Dad! See you tomorrow about six then?"

"Six, it is!" he said, hoping for a hug, but too lazy to get up to get or give one.

Peter was exhausted with Cassandra and Gerald's move, even if most of it involved holding the baby. He had helped to carry their bed, and almost broke his back, but Peter was happy to see that it had opened up a lovely new space in that room upstairs to be filled by…Susan? No, Susan was still living in her own flat. Peter thought of his Hampstead dream, as he waved at the closing front door.

He put on the radio, and out came classical music, easy listening with no words. He picked up the paper and sat back, not particularly looking forward to the day.

There was a lull at work. People had not yet become desperate about where they were going to get the money for all those Christmas presents. They were still basking in the memory of red wine on their holidays in Spain. Soon the credit card bills would come due, and they wouldn't be able to pay them, even with their newer credit cards, because they were also already at the limit.

He refocused on the front page of the newspaper, when, looking down, he noticed a very short paragraph in the corner at the bottom of the page.

"Missing sailboat found! The skeleton of the owner still chained to the boat. Michael Evans, (half-brother of David Evans, who died after falling on his knife in 1956 in Rottingdean), was not really an Evans: Evans was his stepfather's surname. Michael Evans was born Michael Burrows, son of the famous millionaire, Sir Frederick Burrows, who disappeared on a sailboat in the South Pacific in the early thirties. It was said he went down with a boatload of his remaining millions, which he had cashed in and had hoarded after the stock market crash of 1929, (perhaps on purpose, for being rejected by his wife for another wealthy man called Evans). To protect her baby, it was said, his mother had given Michael her current married name which was Evans."

Peter remembered that Michael had quietly mumbled something about liking the name Evans, because it made him feel closer to David.

There was a very quiet moment–for a change. Peter now sat and listened to his inner voice, as he often did. What is life, he mused, lowering his newspaper, but the little things we do every day? Michael ran. David wrote manuscripts. Angela sewed. Peter peered suspiciously over his tea-cups. It was so simple. How had all those philosophers spent their lives writing books about such an easy concept? Peter thought they must have been pushing back the reality of their own lives, as if reading would hold back the moment when it would all be clear that life, indeed, was a simple day-by-day affair. And, when it was over, perhaps they would realize that they might have been running on Hampstead Heath more often than reading fervently. It was as if they were brushing away an annoying shadow that hovered nevertheless over their shoulder, ready to tap it, and say, "It's time."

"No! No!" they might protest. "I'm not ready! I have to finish reading my novel!"

"Yes. Sorry. You are ready. Let's go," the shadow might say. Perhaps all the reading they did was just to avoid the inevitable moment of "good-bye."

Peter stood up, walked down the hallway while admiring his paintings, walked into the kitchen, and put on the kettle. But then he switched it off, as he couldn't quite be bothered to make a cup of tea.

GOING CRAZY

Spring had finally arrived. As he had many times before, Peter began the steep climb up the hill to his mother's house. He left the car at home, as time was not pinching into his morning–for once. The sky was clear, and the day would be warm. Women would be showing their arms by midday, and people would be out and about with errands they had put off during the rainy week.

When he got to the door, he paused, then opened it.

"Hello? Anybody home?" he said, as usual.

There was a silence that alerted Peter immediately, who had not told them he was coming over.

"Hello?" he tried again, walking in and closing the door.

He went into the kitchen and noticed that the back door was wide open.

"Hello?" said Peter.

"Peter! Come here!" shouted Angela from outside of the back door.

Peter sped to the open door and looked out.

"He's fallen, and now he won't wake up!" she spluttered, pointing at Michael.

Peter rushed down the steps to see Michael lying on the ground, out cold, beside a shovel.

"I tried to remind him that Catherine had dug up the cups years ago. It's like he went crazy, insisting they must still be here."

"Father!" shouted Peter, lifting Michael's arm and cradling his shoulder. Michael was unconscious, like he'd hit his head or fainted.

Peter shook him and patted his cheek.

"Peter," mumbled Michael.

"Thank goodness!" said Angela.

"Michael, let's get you up, then!" said Peter, pulling Michael up to a standing position.

"I don't know what happened," said Michael, rubbing his head. "I just blacked out and fell. Am I bleeding?"

Peter searched Michael's head. "No. The ground is soft here–looks like you'll be all right!"

"Come along, Michael," said Angela, "I'll put the kettle on."

Peter helped his father back up the steps and into the house. Once they sat down together at the kitchen table, Peter said, "What were you doing out there, Father?"

"I don't know–a bee in my bonnet," said Michael. "I imagined the six cups were still there. Going mad, I am," he said, rubbing his head. "Well, there might have been something left there. You never know!"

"That's true, Father, but no cups. They're long gone now, back in Italy."

"That's what they say, in that museum with a guard dog."

"No guard dog, but plenty of security," said Peter.

"I don't know that's wrong with me. I feel like those cups were mine. They were mine! I found them, didn't I?"

"They were David's, too," Angela reminded him with a soft smile.

"Yes, but he's not alive to claim them, is he?" said Michael.

"Water under the bridge," said Angela, setting the teacups out.

"Let's leave the past in the past," said Peter.

"Sounding like your mum, Peter!" said Angela.

"Damn! I thought I made that one up!" said Peter.

Michael looked wistfully at the open back door.

"No," said Peter. "You have to leave it, Father. Look what happened just now. It's almost like, if we ever think of those cups, bad things happen. Let's just get on with the present."

"And" added Angela, "leave the past in the past." She poured their tea, and they all took healing gulps, warming their hands on the cups out of habit, although the day was fine and warm.

"You all right, then?" Angela asked Michael.

"'Course not! I'm going crazy, aren't I?"

"A little!" she said.

"A lot!" said Peter.

They all downed their tea, and Angela began pouring second cups.

"Just a little," said Peter, welcoming a full cup anyway.

MICHAEL'S FATHER

Peter dared to hope that life would go back to normal now that the worst had already happened. Surely, nothing else could possibly go awry! Surely it had already been and gone. Once every ten years, perhaps, a family could expect a tragedy, even families that never owned twelve Cellini silver cups!

And besides all that, Peter was tired of the thefts and murders and laws and trials that he witnessed daily in his job. It really was time for another break, this one nice and long.

The Continent called. It always called. Would it always call in some way for as long as he lived? Why didn't South America call, in fact? Or Japan? No, it was Italy and France and even Norway that called once in a while. Perhaps it was just easier to imagine getting there and getting home via train—or even hitchhiking was a possible escape—either direction.

But first, Peter had a few items to cross off his to-do list. He never made a real list, but there was always one just under his conscious self, those inescapable things to do: bills to pay, people to talk to, his car to repair; leaks to patch. The squeaky hinges on the doors had never made it to the top of his mental list—probably never would.

But he could see the light, however dim.

"Turn on the lights, Dad," said Cassandra, wandering in with her baby sleeping in her arms. "You're sitting in the dark again."

"Just musing," he replied.

"Dreaming about the Continent?" she teased.

"You know me well!" He ruffled *The Times,* opened it wide, turned the page, and folded it precisely. He glanced down at the bottom of the third page and was startled to see another article about Michael's father.

"Listen to this!" he said to Cassandra, who stopped in her tracks.

"The missing sunken boat," Peter read, "belonging to Sir Frederick Burrows, has been found off one of the hundreds of small islands in Fiji, and is now in dry dock at the Fiji Royal Suva Yacht Club in the capital town of Suva. Some fragments of skeletal remains of Sir Frederick were found on the boat. It is presumed that he decided to chain himself to his yacht in a storm, so that he would not be thrown into the raging sea. However, there are suspicions that he might have been tied up and robbed by pirates. Authorities are trying to contact Sir Frederick's son, Michael Evans, who is believed to live in Belsize Park in Hampstead, London."

"Well, that's out-of-date information!" Peter mumbled.

"Oh, my God!" said Cassandra.

Like his longing for Hampstead, which had to be crossed off his list, Peter now had to cross off his imagined trip to the Continent. He grabbed his phone and dialed Michael's and Angela's number.

"Dad, sit down first!" he said into his phone.

"I am already sitting down. What's going on?"

"You are not going to believe this," started Peter.

"I already know; they called me last night. What a giant shock! Like you didn't know who your father was, Peter, I never knew my real father, either. They want a DNA test."

"Of course. Shall we meet up?"

"I would love that!"

"Let's meet in your pub at noon."

"Done," said Michael.

Peter hung up and looked at Cassandra.

"Dad?" she said.

"He knew," said Peter.

THE SUNKEN BOAT

The young family climbed up their last few paces to the top of the hill on this abandoned Sussex land, then crept around the old, thatched-roofed cottage. It was surrounded by ash trees and tall green grass.

Daniel pushed the door open, and it complained with a loud creak.

"Hello?" he said. All they could hear was the wind in the trees. He tried again. "Hello?" They leaned in, but all they heard inside was silence.

Daniel invited further squeaking from the door, and his wife and daughter followed him into the cottage.

In a corner, they piled their backpacks, still stuffed with hastily packed pots and pans, a few forks, knives and spoons, tinned spaghetti, bread, tinned baked beans, tomatoes, and a tin of evaporated milk. Lindsey tossed the rotten, crumpled old blankets lying on the large bed onto the floor in the corner. Daniel unloaded their extra baggage of blankets from his back onto the bed.

"Look," said Lindsey, picking up a very brown and white photograph.

Melody stared at the old photograph. "It looks like a sailor on a sail-boat," she said.

"Can you see the name of the sailboat?" her father, Daniel, asked.

"It looks like *Sea Monster*," replied Melody, setting the photograph against the wall on top of a stack of very old and dusty hardbound books.

It would be a cold night if they didn't have wood for the stone fireplace.

"I'll go pick up some kindling," said Lindsey, grabbing the large basket that she found near the hearth.

The clouds were partially covering the sun now, as it set gently over the land, casting long shadows that stretched over the hills. The ocean in the distance had turned a darker color of blue, and the whitecaps were fading and sparkling at the last rays of sun upon them.

Melody followed her mother, picking up the smaller dead twigs and putting them in the basket.

"Why are we staying here tonight, Mum?" she asked.

"I told you, my love. We don't have a home right now, but nobody is living here, so we can live here—possibly for more than one night."

"I like it here, Mum. It's mysterious and lovely. You said there might be elves in the tree stumps, like in books."

Lindsey smiled, remembering all the books they'd had to leave behind when they ran away from the approaching new landlord. She decided to take a trip into the village, where a white-bearded old man owned a tiny second-hand bookshop would be expecting her to visit again one day. He was always kind to her and gave her some very old books for free—with elves and fairies and watercolor illustrations. And now their books were all gone. Someone else would be living in their garden flat—someone who could pay the rent.

"Our basket is full, and the sun has almost set. It's cold. Let's go build a nice warm fire with Daddy and put the kettle on, shall we?"

Lindsey tried to sound cheerful so the child didn't know of her fear of being discovered and being chucked out again. No landlords here though. This little cottage looked abandoned from many years ago. It would do very well for now.

Melody reached for her mother's warm hand, and they walked up their newly-formed path to the cottage.

"Well done," said Daniel, as Lindsey handed the basket to him.

Soon enough, a fire was crackling, and the walls were warming. They huddled as close as was safe, while their fronts were burning, their backs were freezing.

Lindsey filled the tea kettle with the bottled water they'd carried. She made them black tea with a dash of evaporated milk and two teaspoons of lovely white sugar that would feel so good inside their hungry stomachs. Then she placed a hunk of bread in their palms.

Though the sun was quite gone, the sky remained fairly light, as it did all summer. But they went to bed unusually early, cozying up in their own blankets, and keeping warm by hugging each other's clothed bodies for the whole night long.

At around 4 a.m., Lindsey got up quietly, her socks still hugging her cold feet, and though hardly able to open her eyes, she stirred the embers, added some twigs, and put the kettle on for a nice hot cup of tea.

"Mum? Where are we?" asked Melody, yawning and stretching.

"We are in our cozy new home," she said, peaking out the front door at the dawn light, and listening to the chatter of swifts and martins welcoming the day.

As the sun brightened and cast long morning shadows over the hills, Melody circled the cottage and picked some wisteria, two old English red roses, a few dahlias, and a bunch of daisies. She carried them inside to Lindsey, grinning proudly.

"Mum, look what I found around our cottage!"

"They're lovely, Melody. Daddy's gone hunting for a water source, so let's just put them in this watering can with a tiny bit of our water for now."

Melody looked like she felt very clever.

"Found it!" said Daniel, brushing his shoes off outside the front door. "It took a lot of my strength, but after hitting the pipes rather a lot, I got the spigot to budge." He held up a tin bucket of sloshing water.

"Oh, Daddy! You have saved our thirsty flowers!"

Melody carefully scooped out some water and added it to the watering can and her flowers.

"Mum, are we stealing these flowers?"

Lindsey looked up in astonishment. It hadn't occurred to her that Melody could even think that. Flowers belonged to the earth and the earth belonged to everybody. Or did it? Everybody's rain fell on them, after all. It was someone else's property, for sure, but if they obviously never used it, why couldn't they use it and pick the flowers?

"No," said Lindsey. "These are everybody's flowers. They grow everywhere in England. They are ours, then, aren't they?"

"Yes!" said Melody.

Daniel looked at Lindsey, who he knew was telling a white lie.

"It's everybody's sun, and everybody's air, and everybody's water, so they are everybody's flowers that grew with water, sun and air."

Lindsey looked at Daniel. He had forgotten to mention the soil, but that would do for a four-year-old.

"What about the soil, Daddy?"

"Ah," said Daniel. "The soil is the earth, isn't it? We couldn't even walk on it if it were not there. So, it's ours and the flowers', isn't it?"

"Yes!" cried Melody, lying on the quilt that Lindsey had sewn in a nice lady's quilting class in Rottingdean some years before.

They stayed on for weeks. Daniel went down to the village to pick up his benefit income, and shopped for groceries on Lindsey's list: matches, toothpaste, soap, a hand towel, three new toothbrushes, milk, an icepack for the old-fashioned icebox, and an assortment of crackers and biscuits for teatime. And *The Daily Mail*. She wanted to check their horoscopes, even though she thought they were made up by someone trying to make a living with minimal astrology knowledge. She's even thought of applying for the job herself, but she knew absolutely nothing about it. She still loved reading them. It put a ray of hope into her day, especially if Daniel's sign mentioned a good day to apply for work.

The day was hot, and Daniel arrived with his backpack stuffed with her list, including the newspaper. She made him a cup of tea, and he sat down with his hot, steaming cup of tea and *The Daily Mail*. She poured her own tea and sat with him. He automatically handed her the pages with the horoscopes. Melody was talking and playing with elves and fairies just outside the door.

"Look here," said Daniel., "Remember those twelve silver cups that someone had stolen? Well, blimey, they were found at the train station in France in the loo! Fancy that! All the talk at the pub. They're now back in Italy, it says."

Some weeks later, Daniel looked up from that day's newspaper, his mouth wide open. Lindsey noticed that his face was drained almost white.

"What is the matter?" she asked him.

"They found an old, sunken sailboat in the South Pacific. It was English. You won't believe this, but it was called *Sea Monster!*"

SUSSEX

The land in Sussex that the courts granted Michael, which he had inherited legally from his long-dead father, Sir Frederick Burrows, was beautiful, but the house had fallen into disrepair. Michael was thunderstruck that he had inherited it, after the courts found the extenuating circumstances of the honorable drowned owner, Sir Frederick Burrows, could not have paid his taxes, if missing, and then dead. The gold found scattered near the sunken boat was credited towards the taxes.

Michael and Peter drove to the property to see what it was like. The pond had contented swans and ducks in it, and the trees were heavy with chirping birds. The grass was tall and wild, and any paths that had once existed had been covered with weeds and had hardly left a trace. Peter pulled a few of the weeds and found a natural stone path. They trudged together over acres of wild hills and tiny forests of trees.

Michael was delighted.

"But, Peter, my boy," he said, "I'm too old for all this upkeep. I'd like to give it to you before I die."

Peter had just momentarily wished he had such a piece of property, and a flash of hoping Michael would one day leave it to him fluttered through his brain.

They found the stream and worked their way upward until a path seemed to indicate a better route to the top of the hill. In the distance, on the other side of the hills, they could see sheep and cows. The blue sky was sprinkled with fluffy clouds and seemed littered with birds visiting endless trees scattered everywhere.

"How could he leave this beautiful property?" asked Peter.

"He was wealthy," said Michael. "Chances are he'd forgotten he owned it. People who own a lot sometimes do that, you know!"

Peter could not imagine forgetting about this amazing property: another life, another land so different from London, or even Rottingdean. There were villages surrounding the property, rather like the ones he passed by weekly on his train journeys, that Peter noticed looked pretty lively. He had heard about some Americans that had bought cottages around Michael's new property, who mostly came over to stay in England when spring had arrived.

"You want to join these lofty farmers, then?" asked Michael. "Perhaps raise sheep yourself?" Peter saw that Michael had almost laughed at the thought.

"Not me," said Peter. "But think of Henry and Oliver, and even Cassandra and Gerald."

"Now there's a thought. But aren't they desperate to get to the big city?" Michael cautioned, picking up a stone.

"Let's ask. We'll give them a tour and watch their reactions and see who's keen, shall we?"

"Soon! I must complete the signing of the papers with my solicitor shortly. Then we can bring them here." said Michael.

"Soon!" echoed Peter.

"Look! There's a little cabin!" said Michael, pointing up the hill.

They traipsed a little further up to the cabin. Peter approached it, and he couldn't help knocking at the old wooden door, in case anybody was inside.

He heard a rustling from the other side of the door. Peter's eyes widened, and he put his finger to his lips. They listened and waited.

"Who's there?" said a quiet male voice.

"The new owners," said Michael, not unpleasantly.

The door opened a crack, and a young man's face peered out at them.

"We're not here to chuck you out, then," said Michael. "Just walking the property. Would you like to show us around?"

The door opened a bit more and a little girl's face peered out; then a young mother's wide-eyed face stole a look.

"Come in," she said. "I'll put the kettle on."

"No, no! We don't mean to disturb you. This is Peter Evans, my son, and I'm Michael Evans Burrows."

"Ever so pleased to meet you!" she said, cradling her young daughter's head against her shoulder.

"We'll be off then," said Peter.

"No, no!" said the young man. "Please come in. Lindsey's already putting the kettle on!"

They followed the young man inside, sat down all together in some old wooden chairs, and shared a pot of tea. There was no way this little family was going to be asked to leave. There were acres, after all, and the land needed people to continue to tend it.

Peter smiled at Michael as they left. No words needed to be said.

At Last

A week later, Peter walked in through Susan's front door, as she held it open wide, and made a quick study of her face, using the detective skills he had acquired through the years. That eyebrow, slightly elevated, and the blinking of these wonderful eyelashes stumped him.

Peter reached out his hand and took hers. Her eyes remained steady on his. He pulled her up to his chest and cupped his hand around her head, drawing her mouth to his. It was perhaps the longest and most passionate kiss they had yet experienced that encompassed endless longings that they had mostly held back for so long. It seemed like there could only be a sense of eternal certainty between them. Her arms pulled his waist towards her, and he kissed her again, at first a light caress, and then his mouth hardened onto her own welcoming lips.

There was no more discussion needed about moving, or where to move, or what about any of the endless considerations. It was clear now that they had found each other on the same path, moving forward to a happy, peaceful existence.

Peter, of course, had seen too much of life to know there was no "happily ever after." The nature of life was that it was full of inconveniences, misunderstandings, financial and physical hardships, tears, laughter, and sorrow. But as long as they could live together, which that kiss and hug spelled out like they were a permanent statue, they would be content, offering each other tea, advice and a listening ear. It even occurred to Peter, who had been considering it for a long time, that he might now ask her to marry him.

They drew apart, but still held each other's arms, looked into each other's eyes–both full of possibilities, and Susan said, "Peter, do you think we should get married?"

Peter burst out laughing. "You clever devil! You beat me to it!"

"I'll take that as a 'yes'!"

"Yes! Yes! Yes!" Peter yelled, dropping his bag on the floor and picking her up and swinging her around. He put her down and gave her a sweet, sealing kiss, then leaned down to get his bag, and grabbed his back and groaned.

"What is it, darling?" asked Susan.

"A twinge only," said Peter. "Not to worry!"

"A cup of tea?" she offered predictably. Yes, he wouldn't mind a cup of tea. They went into the kitchen, and he watched her pour from the larger teapot, and he almost choked with happiness to have her offering him a nice hot cup of tea.

THE MOVE

Susan and Peter sat down in her jumbled flat in Rottingdean.

"We're going to keep tossing or storing all our stuff, until we can fit into Michael's flat, aren't we?" Susan said.

"I'm just bringing my penny whistle and my underwear," Peter said. "I can leave all the furniture and paintings in the house for now–for the kids. So, Susan, just fill up the flat with your things. I love your paintings, and you do have decent taste in furniture. I especially love your kitchen table and chairs."

There was a lull in the conversation. Then Susan said, "Are you absolutely sure about all this, Peter? It's such a gigantic move for both of us, isn't it?"

"Very, very sure, my love."

Susan reached over and touched Peter's cheek. Peter realized, as his skull tingled with her light touch, that happiness was just sitting this close, and all he had to do was acknowledge it to himself, without question. All he had to do was stop holding his breath. He sighed and raised his hand and put it on top of Susan's. He could hardly stand his own happiness and contentment. Why had they waited so long?

"It isn't about the furniture, is it, my love?" asked Susan.

"It's about this very moment, yes, it's about almost crying with this late-in-the-day coming together. I admit, I feel warm and cozy right inside my whole body, from my heart." Peter kept his hand on hers and leaned towards her. He knocked his teacup over on the way, and it spilled onto the tray.

"Never mind," he said, but swore softly, anyway. He kept leaning towards her, putting his arm around her head, and pulling her towards his lips, and kissing her with passion. They parted and looked lovingly into each other's eyes.

"We are the luckiest people in the world," Susan said.

"It took a while," Peter laughed, leaning back, and placing his palm right into the puddle of tea by his sideways cup.

Susan smiled, set the cup to rights, and put a handy serviette on top of the puddle.

"Another cup?" she asked with her loving smile.

THE WEDDING

Counting the hours until the wedding, Peter was excited in a way that interrupted his own normal calmness in the face of something earth-shattering. He spent too much time checking his bowtie in the mirror and wishing he had not had his hair cut so short. He hoped there might be half a chance he would look somewhat like his usual long-fringed self. So, his floppy, blond fringe in the front had been preserved by his last-minute wishes at the barber's. As he took one last glance at his teeth and tested his smile, he walked out of the bathroom in the Hampstead flat into the sitting room and sat down. Michael came from the kitchen with a mug of coffee for each of them.

"You sure of this, mate?" teased Michael with a wink.

"Never surer in my life. But I do admit to some kind of jitters, Father. It's a big decision."

They finished their coffee and walked out the door, up the hill and down the street to the Belsize Park Town Hall. Susan had not yet arrived.

"She's probably forgotten," teased Michael.

"Ah! There she is!" said Peter, pointing towards her parked car.

When she got out of the car, Peter could see that Susan was wearing a white dress that went almost down to her ankles. It was her mother's, apparently. She wore her hair in ringlets down her back and her lips were faintly red. Her eyes seemed dark and mysterious. Peter hardly recognized them. But all that mascara did seem to add to her beauty. He felt his heart thumping a bit too much and put his hand on his chest to feel it. It was even a little painful–indigestion, he figured. Excitement! Anticipation!

Angela walked by Susan's side, and behind them came Henry, Oliver, and Cassandra, who was pushing the pram. Then Lawanda appeared with her husband, who was pushing another pram.

Everybody climbed the steps up to the door and filed into the Town Hall with quiet nods and happy smiles. Susan's small family from afar arrived and sat on the bride's side. It was to be quiet and informal, but it was perfect for Peter, who hated a fuss.

Peter's grown children were making gestures that he could see, like thumbs up and blowing kisses. The two young mothers must have drugged the toddlers–one could hope!

It was quick–almost too quick. All that fuss for a few words and signatures, a kiss, and a handshake with the white-haired minister, and then there they were, lining up along the wide steps of the Town Hall in rows, smoothing their hair, and smiling for the camera.

Lunch was catered at the restaurant across the street. In the midst of much laughter and wine, Peter caught Angela's eyes, which looked rather teary to him. Michael offered her his handkerchief after dabbing his own eyes.

Lawanda reached into her bag and brought out a large gift for Susan and Peter. Very mysterious! Peter did not want to open it right there, but everybody insisted. Susan took the red ribbon off, and Peter unwrapped the crinkly paper around the box.

"I got it at the museum. I just couldn't resist it!" said Lawanda, rubbing her hands together.

Inside the box there were twelve tiny reproductions of Cellini's silver cups, complete with astrological engravings.

"Not real, of course," said Lawanda.

"I hope not," spluttered Peter, as Susan took one out to examine it.

Peter felt his heart beating too fast again.

Not real, he said to himself.

I'M RUNNING

It was clear now that Michael had not been well for a few weeks—not well at all. A few months after his crazy search for the cups, the family now all stood around Michael's bed with somber faces.

Peter looked at Michael, grown so thin, with his stubby, unshaven chin, and his half-closed eyes. Peter had suspected that Michael was dying, though it was hard to admit it to himself these past weeks.

"What matters the most," Michael said, his voice cracked and weak, "is that we all forgive each other. I'm the first one hoping to be forgiven. I was born with a very active mind, with my keen eye for valuable antiques, and how I saw the value of those silver cups. I can't help being a little different." He looked at Angela and at his family surrounding him in their large bed.

Peter took Michael's hands. "Father, I found you, and I found myself. You have, indeed, been a trial in a few ways for me, as I might have been for you, but I have learned to forgive you, of course."

"I know I'm dying. The doctor said I've got pneumonia—otherwise, why would you all be standing here around my bed? You should be outside. It's a lovely day. I'm old. I've had a long life. I'm a great-grandfather now."

"Do you have any regrets?" asked Oliver, in his usual forward manner.

Michael looked around at all these people leaning in towards him.

"Well, perhaps one regret."

They all leaned in even more.

"I wish I hadn't demanded the other six silver cups from David that day I went by to visit him–instead of us fighting, and him slipping and falling on his knife." Michael's voice was almost a whisper now. "I regret that we didn't work it out better. I could have also just left and not been so greedy. I see that now. Silly! Imagine losing David over a bit of silver. We always fought, you know. But I loved my brother, didn't I?" said Michael, tearing up.

"Don't cry, Grandpa," said Cassandra.

"Who's crying?" Michael said, as she dabbed his tears away.

Michael's eyes closed halfway, and he fell into a state of reverie. There was a profound silence as Peter looked around at his children and grand-child, and then back at Michael.

"I'm running!" Michael's weakened voice said. "Come with me, Peter. Let's go for a run on Hampstead Heath. Shouldn't you be in school? Never mind. This is our chance, isn't it? Let's run together, my boy, my nephew, David's son," he whispered. "I'm running...."

"*Your* son," whispered Peter.

"My son...."

Michael's eyes were closing, and his breathing was rough. He strained to open his eyes one last time. Peter took Michael's hands and kissed them. He thought he saw Michael smile and then, as Michael's eyes fluttered and then closed, it seemed that he had gone away, run into the clouds–exuberant, looking for those cups that would somehow elude his final grasp–but running, perhaps, towards David, who stood waiting, holding his Cellini manuscript, ready to continue the fight.

"He's gone," Peter said, holding Angela close. He wiped his eyes again and again, but try as he might, he could not stop the warm, salty tears running down his cheeks.

NEXT

The effect on the entire family standing around Michael was positively traumatic. With Michael went all his stories for over fifty years. It was like, as his eyelids closed, the stories evaporated, and quite disappeared through the window into the sky–into the ether, out into space–into the nothingness of not mattering.

Angela sat bereft, handkerchief dabbing her eyes and nose, and her mind the last one containing those secrets and stories that Michael may have confided to her. Perhaps none of it was important now. Certainly, nobody was going to dash off to Italy and frighten Peter and his children. Peter was devastated to see his father, his real father, disappearing into the land of silence. No more walks on Hampstead Heath or on the cliffs; no more pats on the back; no more confessions of one man to another; no more hints of family history that still made Peter lie awake at night.

Angela's handkerchief was soaked through. Peter offered her his large white handkerchief while trying to make his own tears stay put. She covered her eyes and nose with it, and a sob poured out from behind it.

Henry took Peter's arm and leaned on Peter's shoulder, staring at Michael. Cassandra laid her sleeping baby down on the large bed, came up behind Peter to link his other arm, and put her head on his other shoulder.

The only thing that made it tolerable was the length of time in be-tween, where they could enjoy each other, and deny that death would one day happen again in the distant future. Nobody knew who was next. Peter looked at Michael, white and still. Was Angela next? Nobody knew. One thing Peter felt, however, was that it would be a natural death. The silver cups were locked away in the country of their origin, so that story must finally be at an end. No more cliff deaths, or knife deaths, or air-plane accidents or people wrongly sent to jail for twelve years. Hopefully, the next death would be peaceful, like Michael's here. Peter even hated thinking about it, but witnessing this possibility, gave him hope that if it were Angela's turn, she would leave the world peacefully, perhaps with a slight smile, a sense of gratitude for all the good things in her life, and love in her eyes, as she looked, one-by-one, at her son and his children and her great-grandchild. Now that would be a perfect death, Peter thought.

A QUESTION

Months before he died, Michael had given notice to his Hampstead tenants, and they had moved out two months before Peter and Susan's marriage at the registry office at the Belsize Park Town Hall. Michael told Peter he had also added a nice wad of money to help the tenants with their inevitable reluctance to go.

Henry, Oliver, and their University friends remained in Peter's house, where Peter, of course, was invited any time for a cup of tea. On weekends, they often spent time walking Michael's, now Peter's, Sussex property.

Susan sold or stored her extra furniture. It was such a painful process that it was a miracle their relationship was intact after the move. But it remained intact, indeed! And two happy people now lived in Hampstead and had finally married each other.

"Peter, darling," said Susan, one morning in bed.

"Yes, my love," he answered.

"I would love a dog," she said, cuddling up to him.

"A what? A dog?"

"Yes. I love dogs," she said, kissing his cheek.

"But how will we travel?" he protested.

"The children will look after it, won't they?"

Peter looked at his new wife. He could not say no. He tried to think of reasons why it was a silly idea. But he could not. Truth to tell, he also loved dogs. He would really love walking their dog on nearby Hampstead Heath.

"Small or large," he asked.

"Small enough to take on an airplane."

"Done!"

BAD LUCK

Peter kept waking up from eternal dreams, where the Cellini silver cups were lined up lovingly in the middle of his long kitchen table back in Rottingdean. He would open his eyes in a sweat, and realize it was a dream, and then count his blessings that the cups were out of his family's lives.

One night, in their comfortable Hampstead abode, Susan was jolted awake, and sat straight up beside Peter in bed, and began screaming.

"Susan, wake up!" he comforted her. "It's only a dream!"

"It's crashed!" she yelled, throwing her arms around Peter. He saw himself back at the airport, handing Jeannie's handkerchief to Susan. Then he imagined fading away into death and wondered grudgingly, as he wiped his eyes, if the bad luck from the cups was still invading their lives.

"Oh, Peter, so sorry!" she spluttered.

"It's only a dream," he comforted her again.

"It felt so real, Peter! Do you think we might still be having bad luck because of those cups?"

Peter touched his chin, felt the night's growth, brushed his stubble and said, "The cups are back in Italy now. We shall never have bad luck anymore."

"But look what happened! A plane crash, Peter!"

"But the cups were in Italy by then, weren't they?"

They both nodded in the morning light.

"That must mean," said Susan, cocking her head, "that the plane crash was not at all bad luck caused by those cups!"

Peter had lived most of his life with this superstition intact, and he admitted to himself that it was going to be quite a challenge for him to give it up.

"Just bad luck, then?" he asserted, punching his pillow.

"Perhaps just ordinary bad luck, Peter."

Peter could still hardly imagine this possibility. Everything bad that had ever happened throughout his whole life, he attributed in some way to the Cellini cups. He knew that he had figured out that the cups had always needed to be back in Italy where they belonged, before all their lives could change for the better.

Peter had finally finished reading David's Cellini manuscript and had handed it to Henry to read. Peter knew, deep in his being, that he had become, in some sense, the guardian of the cups, the person destined to make sure they remained permanently housed back in Italy. It was as if Benvenuto Cellini had spoken to Peter, from five hundred years before, about Cellini's own lifelong yearning for the cups that were his supreme achievement, to be returned to Florence.

"Peter," said Susan, turning over in their bed to face him as the dawn light from the window exposed his thoughtful face.

"Yes, Susan, my love?"

"We won't ever have to worry again about this superstition, will we?"

Peter felt a pain in his chest and placed his hand over it.

"What's the matter, Peter?" said Susan, alarmed, and sitting up.

"It hurts right here!" he said, patting his heart.

"Is it your heart?" she asked.

"Do you think...?" he said, listening hard and feeling his heart thumping.

"Of course!" she said. "The cups are not in our lives, remember?"

"Yes, but...."

"No, Peter. Even if it's a heart attack (which it isn't), it's nothing to do with those horrible cups, is it?"

"They're not horrible cups! But sorry, Susan. I see that this superstition has got to stop," said Peter, now fully awake. "Let's stop it together, Susan, right now, shall we?"

Peter sat up, a smile creeping across his face.

"It's gone," he said, his voice high, breathing easily again and rubbing his chest.

"Indigestion," she said, rather on the loud side.

"Alright! Alright!" said Peter. "No more superstitious conclusions! I agree, this is all completely ridiculous! The truth is," he added somewhat bravely, defying the gods, "It's not the fault of the cups, is it? It's all just bloody normal bad luck–and indigestion!"

Peter laughed and turned towards the warmth and the vanilla ice cream smell of his dear wife Susan, embracing her with the deep love that he had found again–at last.

And yet, as he bent to kiss her, he glanced at the wall and could swear he saw a madman on a horse, with his bloody sword swinging, his eyes glaring, his horse charging the crowd, and his curse loud and violent. And then Peter imagined an urchin and his father, and a horse and cart, making their way to some Italian port.

He closed his eyes and sighed, as he embraced Susan with a gentle fervor, and kissed her welcoming mouth. It was over.

It was finally over.

CELLINI–1571

Cellini lies dying in a castle, and he is now famous beyond anyone (besides Michelangelo) in centuries, surrounded by wealthy patrons, admirers and politicians. Although he is dying, he inwardly smiles to himself. He has accomplished the most exquisite art and sculpture ever made, and he knows it. His drawing is unmatched; his sculpture is daunting, and he thinks of his nearly ten years of loving labor finishing his bronze statue of Perseus. His fame is worldwide. Yes, he regrets his temper and how it got out-of-hand at times–but only for good causes. No guilt there. They asked for it–they deserved it! He knows, as his breathing becomes labored, that he has lived a free man (albeit often in jail or on the run from the law). He had thrived and survived by murdering the right people and getting pardoned and praised for it.

He remembers back in 1546, upon his return from five years working under King Francis I, when he was just delivering that one magnificent cup to d'Este. It was a period of riches, of fame, and, of course, a time when half the world loved him. The other half were clearly just jealous and narrow-minded.

His breathing becomes more labored, as he remembers that irksome little cart and horse that he had galloped by, and his endless niggling feeling that somehow, they were involved in the disappearance of his twelve silver cups. He jerks his shoulder as he lies in his bed and imagines how he overlooked them both times he had seen them. It was intuition, but he'd been in such a fury and a hurry, that it took all the rest of his life to realize how his hunches were usually right. He remembers how he asked that captain of the galleon if he knew anything about his cups, while Cellini's horse had sweated and pranced in place. Cellini never knew that his apprentice, Caruso, was on that ship, and Cellini never knew that Caruso had tried to wave at him from the crow's nest. He never knew that, by the time Caruso had signaled from the crow's nest and started to shout, Cellini and his horse were galloping away in a furious cloud of dust.

Cellini would never know. And he would never know if the cups would ever be seen again, or if they had gone to the bottom of the ocean on that ship that people had said was never found.

There is, most likely, less than a quarter of an hour left of his life to contemplate. All he has is his racing mind, while his body is lying there, as still as marble. He can feel his own life disappearing and imagines drawing a huge picture of his body, its length on the bed, a sort of languishing posture, falling away from the nerves of life, with a look of resignation on his face—yet, his eyes, so wide—showing an endless search for beauty, meaning, and an eternal—what? An eternal curse on those who will suffer until his precious silver cups are returned to Florence. He will never see them, he knows, but they might endure, perhaps, and someone might carry them back to his beloved Florence for the world to admire. He imagines, in his final breaths, that the cups were still, in fact, on that galleon and had somehow not gone to the bottom of the sea but ended up in another country. Wasn't she bound for England?

"Whoever keeps my silver cups," Cellini swears aloud, his voice fading, "Will have bad luck all their lives until they are returned to Florence!" This curse is overheard by the highly esteemed and wealthy crowd surrounding his bed: high church superiors, politicians, friends and admirers, who lean in to hear these last words. They know that sometimes the final wishes of a dying person might contain the elements of revenge that continue forever—until their wishes are satisfied.

Cellini slumps into death with a devilish smile, expressing finality. He knows his curse will work, although he always thinks of himself as a man slightly above superstition.

His smile fades away as he stops breathing, but perhaps, as he dies, the curse is rising into the sky and will remain until the cups are returned to Florence at last, and Cellini's revenge is fulfilled.

The End

THE CURSE OF THE CURSE

For what is stolen, must be returned.

A country claims the great art of its citizens, no matter how far back in the centuries it goes. Think of the African sculptures that were spirited off to Europe and North America. The owners want them returned. Think of ancient Greek artifacts from two centuries ago, stolen over years, sold and resold. Think of the labor of slaves stolen and never repaired. Think of the years a black person in the USA could not buy a house, especially a house in a nice neighborhood full of white people. Think of all the women for years and years, who were held back from publication because they were women. These things are thefts and need reparations. My point is, until they are repaired, they remain stolen, and the people who do not return them will also continue to suffer. That was all Cellini wanted in this fictitious story: He wanted his cups returned to Italy, even when he knew it might happen after his death.

People who steal are punished with their guilt, which affects them whether they realize it or not. A stolen painting or sculpture has a red light around it, yelling, "Give me back!" The art treasures that Hitler stole are still being traced and returned to this day, with lawyers crossing continents to fight for their return to the rightful families of the original owners in the original countries. Each return of an art piece produces a sigh of relief, both for the new owners and the original family's heirs.

241

Each apology to the descendants of slaves is greeted with a sigh of relief and tears by the descendants. It makes the politician saying it sigh with relief. It seems so fragile, just a few words of honesty and recognition about the horror of what was done for so long. As we well know, words have power.

In the end, people do have bad luck, even through no fault of their own. But I ask you, is it bad luck for the people who died of the COVID virus, or is it because of someone who decided it was a hoax? Each action or word carries meaning and has repercussions for centuries. That is why, in *Cellini's Revenge*, all the stories through the centuries are blended into an event five hundred years previously. Each action has a reaction. Some call it Karma. Each theft has endless repercussions. Each return has reactions, and the pain is lifted. It is all up to us, and it is all possible.

ABOUT THE AUTHOR

Wendy Bartlett currently lives in Berkeley, California. She lived in England for thirteen years and visits her family regularly where she haunts the places she writes about like the Old Bailey, the River Thames and Rottingdean. She re-published her novel *Broad Reach* in 2019 and has published four children's books recently, including the popular children's novel: *The Flood*. The new edition of *Cellini's Revenge, The Mystery of the Silver Cups, Book 1* was published in 2020, followed soon after by *Book 2*. This one is *Book 3*, the last of the trilogy.

Coming soon is Wendy's next novel, derived from her screenplay, *Girl with a Violin,* which will be published as an audiobook, as well as paperback and ebook editions.

Wendy has written much poetry and nine books. She is excited to work on her writing every day, telling great stories.

The Elizabeth Books
Written and Illustrated by Wendy Bartlett
Available through Indiebound.org, bookshop.org, Apple Books, Nook, and Kobo
as well as other print and ebook retailers worldwide

A beautifully illustrated book for children attending pre-school showing all the activities children do in preschool: meeting new friends, listening to stories, swinging on the tire swing, playing table games, singing with a guitar, hammering, riding bikes, and playing in the sand. Teachers, parents, and children will love this book because they can point and say, "We go to a school like that!"

First grade is a challenge with new friends, maybe a new teacher and a feeling of advancement into the world of reading and writing. It is a time of friendship, sharing, learning and playing. It is a place where children come into their own, a secure leap into the world of math and science, and the beginning of learning to spell and sound out whole sentences. It is fun!

My mother sketches me all over Paris, whether of me eating an ice cream cone under the Eiffel Tower, or washing socks in the bidet, or going on the merry-go-round. It is lots of fun being her model! It takes many turns for me on the merry-go-round for her to finish her drawing. I don't mind a bit! Paris is amazing!

When eleven-year-old Elizabeth is left to babysit her four-year-old sister one rainy night, neither of them expect the adventure that unfolds. Their parents don't return home, and by morning there is a flood that fills the first floor of their house. Elizabeth must take initiative and make an agonizing decision: whether to stay put where her parents might find them, or to be brave and leave home to go in search of their parents. Dangers loom in either scenario.

With her only child off to college, Sarah, a divorcée, is overwhelmed with emptiness. Here home overlooking San Francisco Bay is quiet, and her work with young children is routine. Most of all, her heart has become an excruciating vacuum.

When she meets a very sexy and charming Englishman tending his sailboat, Sarah makes an impulsive decision. It takes little to persuade her to join this mysterious sailor for an around-the-world cruise as his second mate, despite her amateur knowledge of sailing.

At first, warm winds, lust, and romance fill her days as they journey to the South Pacific. Soon her romantic idyll is rocked by the stormy seas as the dark side of her captain is revealed against the harsh backdrop of sailing. As life on the water becomes unforgiving, Sarah finds herself plunged into an abyss of fear and confusion, and ultimately, the greatest challenge she has ever faced.

Broad Reach *is engaging, real and powerful. While most sailing stories romanticize the experience, this gripping novel explores the hard, cold, nitty-gritty, crazy-making, dark side of small-boat ocean cruising. A must read!*
—**William McGinnis, author of *Sailing the Greek Islands, Whitewater: A Thriller, Gold Bay, The Guide's Guide, Whitewater Rafting* and more.**

COMING SOON

A famous 18-year-old fiddle player, Beau, is abducted from her parents' huge Sierra home at a birthday folk jam in her honor one summer in the early part of the 21st century. As a fire burns up the mountain while she is buried on the land under a pile of brush, she is found just in time.

A month later, much to her horror, she is abducted again, this time from a Berkeley music jam. The culprit – a crazy but brilliant classical violinist only known for his expert folk guitar playing – hides her away in an underground room in the Sierras so he can compel her to learn classical violin.

Pale, gaunt and shattered, can she escape?

Cellini's Revenge

Book Club Questions

1. What was your favorite part of the book?

2. Which scene stuck with you most?

3. What surprised you about the book?

4. If you could ask the author anything, what would it be?

5. Did this book remind you of Cellini's Revenge, Book 1, or Book 2?

6. Did this book strike you as original?

7. Which characters did you like best?

8. How did the settings impact the story?

9. Could this book also be a standalone?

LETTER TO MY READERS

Thank you very much for reading my novel, *Cellini's Revenge: The Mystery of the Silver Cups, Book 3*.

I appreciate your interest and hope you found it as exciting and fun to read as it was to write.

I would so appreciate your taking a moment to please write to me at wendyberk@aol.com and let me know what you think.

If you would like, you could also write an honest review wherever you bought this book online, like Amazon. Here's a direct link to my author page on that site. amazon.com/author/wendybartlett. Just click on the red *Cellini's Revenge* cover.

If you missed *Book 1* or *Book 2*, you can find them through the above link, and do keep an eye out for *Girl with a Violin*, which I will be publishing soon. If you would like to be on the advance notice list for any of my future writings, please go to my website and sign up.

Thank you very much again for reading my novel.

Gratefully,

Wendy Bartlett

Wendy Bartlett, author
wendybartlett.com